Grave Witness

Grave Witness

PETER LEVI

St. Martin's Press
New York

For Deirdre

Library of Congress Cataloging in Publication Data

Levi, Peter.
   Grave witness.

   I. Title.
PR6023.E912G69   1985   823'.914   85-11839
ISBN 0-312-34452-X

First published in Great Britain by Quartet Books Ltd.

1

'That is,' observed my colleague Frowser with some relish, 'hot ice and wondrous strange snow.' I caught him sneaking a glance to see that I was baffled, before he turned his whole attention to the soufflé. We were talking about how some foods, like eggs, which Frowser prefers, invite paradoxical cooking, and other food, like beef, which I prefer, likes to remain its simple self. I am not sure when the old rule I was brought up on fell out of general use. You were supposed never to discuss food at table, particularly not the food you were eating. Come to think of it, I don't know who ever observed that rule. Certainly in my college everyone talks about cooking, and the same goes for both my marriages.

I hate Frowser with an almost dispassionate contempt. He reminds me of an even older, scalier monster called Grimble whom I truly hated. Sometimes I think Grimble never really died. Maybe he survived his adventurous death in the Balkans by peasant remedies, and avoided the second death of his evil reputation by simply reappearing as Frowser in his old college. The dates fit, and Frowser has a furtive air and a highly improbable moustache. The reference books credit Frowser with a critical volume called *Sentiment and Metaphor*. I have heard it said that his chapter on Gertrude of Wyoming opened the eyes of the learned world to new delicacies in the shorter longer poems of the earlier middle century. But I have never seen that book.

A simple archaeologist can avoid most kinds of claptrap. Our darkness needs no candles. The worst of my early spring sufferings was dining that night in Oxford, and in someone

1

else's college, because of a committee. Bachelors and the ex-married are suckers for committees, and on this one I sat with Frowser. It was a committee for republishing old scholarly works of classical interest and literary merit. I had been fighting hard since tea-time for Thomas Hobbes's translation of Thucydides, and against his translation of Homer. Homer is by my lights the best poet but not in that version. Frowser was now purple in the face with prejudice and soufflé Grand Marnier. But I played a waiting game. The port would turn him port-coloured. If at that stage I allowed him Wood's *Observations on Homer*, he might allow me Wood's *Palmyra in the Desert*.

I was punished for my deviousness. Over the nuts I was cornered by an expert on moated granges with a perfectly polished bald head.

'Palmyra,' he said. 'Hrraa hmph.'

'Yes,' I said. 'In the desert. Do you know it?'

'No. Hrraa. Are you that Ben Jonson?'

Flattery is my downfall. One of the most moving stories I know is that of a very old scholar from Oxford travelling to Germany by train in the days when that meant foot-warmers and plaid rugs, and modestly sending in his card at a library in Berlin. They said, '*Ihre Name ist bekannt*', 'Your name is well known here', and the old man wept with pleasure. Of course I blushed and said yes I had written about Palmyra in the past. I was interested in the Greeks outside Greece, in how far they penetrated.

'Well, I have, hmph, an old neighbour. In the country you know. Might be glad of your help. Advice you know. Of course, hraa. Of course he's as obstinate as a Macedonian mule. Used to run a Macedonian mule-train in fact, in the fourteen war. Hraa, hmph. I've always thought that must have been rather a meeting of minds. Hraa. Lives in a fifteenth-century monastic grange. Moated. Old now of course. And as I say, hmph. Obstinate. Obstinate.'

'What use could I be? I'm no expert on medieval moats.'

'Oh no.' He was shocked by that. 'Oh no, quite so. Not the thing anyway. Can you credit it? He has it filled with damned daffodils. And the moat's earlier than the house. Obstinate, as I say. In his eighties. Hmph. Finding things. Said he'd like to talk to you about it.'

'Where's he finding things?'

'Oh, in his grounds. In his grounds. Somewhere beyond the tennis court. Bit suspect, I shouldn't wonder. Hmph. Nuts?' I wrestled with an unbreakable college walnut, and he went on: 'Might interest you to see the house though. Has some good rooms. Bit over-stuffed with things. Hraa. Photographs of the mules and so on. The Serbian campaign. Name's Ralph Iggleby. Lives out beyond Blenheim. Hrmph. Hrrmph.'

At this moment we were interrupted by being sucked into the conversation going on across the polished table. What with the heat of the fire, the gleaming bald heads, the shining mahogany and the glittering silver, the wine had begun to swim gently upwards into my eyes, and the candle-flames were dancing.

'The kind of pig,' Frowser was glaring at me, 'who claims to read writers for their prose style. Hobbes's Thucydides instead of the *Leviathan*. Might as well be reading the later writings of Henry James.' This gratuitous insult got home to me. Henry James was one of the few writers I had once consciously reserved for middle age; so far he was one of its greatest disappointments. 'His cheek.'

'His cheek,' I muttered scornfully, 'was redolent of the matutinal steel.'

'You see what I mean,' said Frowser in malevolent triumph. 'Mere frippery. Not scholarship. That isn't criticism.'

I ground my teeth and drank some more.

Frowser went on. 'Did I hear you speak about Ralph Iggleby? What have you got to do with him?'

'I was hearing about him. He has a moat full of daffodils.'

Fortune, as Philip Sidney once observed in the middle of a battle, was tired of running up and down on one side of the bloody tennis court. She deserted Frowser, and the moated grange expert came to my rescue.

'Not the true English daffodil, Frowser. Hraa. Not the wild yellow one. Hrrmph. Have to go to Gloucestershire for that. Hrmm. Nowadays.'

'I thought they made a finer show than ever this year,' said Frowser.

3

'What, Frowser? What? In the moat, Frowser? Do you mean in the moat? You like them?' It was 'Hraa, Hraa!' among the trumpets. I comforted myself with kiwi fruit, and gradually, as happens sometimes in the course of long dinners, I recovered my sobriety.

Outside, the cloisters were as virginal and shadowy as they always had been. A thin swarm of stars hung in the upper air. It was time to find a taxi and be driven out into the country to my beloved, untidy cottage and its cold windows and overgrown orchard. Grey stone and lichen flowered and died in our headlights. There was no one about as I abandoned the world for another night, and fitted my key to the front door. Nobody used to lock doors in villages, everyone was on first-name terms, but nowadays people no longer know one another's names, and there are stories of the loss of an axe or a saw or the lid of a dustbin. In spite of that fact, on which I often sadly brood, it was an innocent night smelling of spring, with a faint, delicious undertone of bonfires. Dinner had slipped out of my mind; Oxford might have been a thousand miles away. Tomorrow's newspaper might have recorded the sinking of the *Titanic*. I drew the bedroom curtains.

Next morning I was woken by the telephone at three minutes after nine. An aged voice I had never heard before, as smooth and grainy as a river pebble. Was it Doctor Jonson? Yes, he thought there was no mistake. Had he disturbed me? No? Being a light sleeper himself he was never sure. And nowadays of course. But he wanted to catch me. Yes, good, good. Could I come over to lunch one day this week? Any day? It wasn't far. In fact we were near neighbours. And fellow members of the Society of Antiquaries. Fellows, in fact, fellow fellows. Yes. He'd therefore presumed to telephone. Hadn't disturbed me? Good, good. Disliked writing notes. Had no one to deliver them. The list of fellows gave no phone numbers, but with the phone book of course, no trouble. Early in the week then? However early I liked. Well, even today. If I liked. We could get down to something. Oh yes his name. Iggleby. Ralph Iggleby. Lived at Stonehouses. Yes, not far at all. Expect me half past twelve. Did I like claret? One has to ask nowadays. Fellow the other day drank whisky all through dinner. Anxious to consult me. Yes. Matter had cropped up. Open it and let it breathe.

The phone went dead. Sleep had retreated to the back of my head where it spends all day long waiting to pounce. He seemed a polite old man. As one might say a clean old man. The claret was a good sign. I thought of all the cold cellars of claret in houses anywhere between Oxford and northern Scotland, the wine as cold as those long ago rainstorms that once nourished the soil where the vines grew. I thought of the under-heated rooms and the dark bottles with cool cheeks rushed upstairs when the soup was steaming. If I had to choose I would settle for tepid food and breathing wine. Having drunk as much champagne out of tin mugs as most people, I find in my mellowing days that what I like most about wine is its innocent ceremoniousness.

The old man's house was made of very old brick with stone windows. It stood in a park behind the remnants of a bold double avenue of lime trees, just in early leaf.

The flowers in the depression which must once have been a moat were paper-white narcissi. Half of the front of the house itself, which was not very big, was smothered under a magnolia grandiflora, unconquerably healthy, and catching at the light like a huge laurel tree. Herbs grew in cracks and crevices near the door. The bell clanged like doom and a maid admitted me into a stone-flagged, cavernous hall crowded with umbrellas and fishing-rods and the heads of foxes and others. She led me to the door of a long, dark library where a tall, dark-suited figure was bending down to stare through a magnifying glass at a tray of bits and pieces. He straightened with a youthful grin. His face was fresh, his eye glinted, his hair was white and brushed straight across.

'I'm Iggleby. You Dr Jonson? You found us? She let you in? I never hear that bell. Come and look at this.'

The tray was full of crumbs and fragments of bone, a few teeth, and one big piece of human skull. With a mixture of excitement and reverence he handed me the magnifying glass. To me a tooth enlarged is still a tooth. Indeed, I am probably the last archaeologist left alive who believes that the bones of the dead should be left to rest in the earth. But a host is a host.

5

'Nice bit of skull,' I said.

'*Very* nice,' he replied. 'And the teeth.'

'Are they all from one skeleton?'

'Oh I think so. Oh yes I think so. From the cow pasture. Edge of the old deer park, you know.'

'Freshly excavated?'

'Oh no. Early days. I dug there in the school holidays when I was eleven. Not so recent as it used to be. Evans taught me you know.'

'Not Arthur Evans?'

'Old Sir John Evans, Arthur's father. Very encouraging, he was. Been digging ever since, yes, one way and the other.'

'Have you ever published any of it?'

'Oh I think that's a fearful mistake, don't you? Sherry? Pale or this? People constantly prying into one's things, crossing one's land. Heaven knows what. Bad enough as things are. Do you know I had a damn fellow in here tried to make me grub up the narcissi out of my moat? Disturbing the ground, he said. Called them daffodils. Another fellow worse still, fellow the vicar brought. Called them daffs. Can you imagine? Awful fellow called Frowser. No, fearful mistake publishing. Might get read by some damn preservationist. The old Duke of Marlborough gave me that advice. Great-grandfather to this one, he must have been. Of course it wasn't preservationists in his day, hikers it used to be. And that damn hunt. I won't let them through here. Disturb my excavations. More sherry? Good. Take it with us. Chilly in the dining room.'

As he showed me through he grew confidential. There was a place where he had the wall stripped down to reveal an inner stony structure, rubble to the uninitiated. 'Twelfth-century,' he said, tapping it affectionately. 'This house is listed, supposed to be fifteenth-century, but there's something much better underneath. Twelfth-century rubble walling, think of that. I get at it on the quiet. I've explored most parts. Can't stand fifteenth-century architecture, can you? And these windows. Such a boring light. I'd like to put in Burne-Jones windows, like peering out through trees. But quite hard to get you know. And of course there'd be a row. Someone would be certain to notice. Letters to the paper. Council for the Preservation of God

Knows What. Our heritage, they call it you know. Appalling cheek really.'

Lunch was highly unexpected. It was genuine well-hung mutton with onion sauce. The mashed potatoes arrived in the belly of a pink and white Chinese porcelain goose. The claret was a Pauillac, from that long tongue of gravel that screens Bordeaux from the Atlantic. I think it was Haut-Bages or Croizet-Bages, and he told me with some glee that it was 1970. By two in the afternoon I was ready for anything and we were friends for life. I think now that old Ralph Iggleby took me on in the same wholehearted way as he was drinking up his seventy claret. He was not going to see many more autumns or many more springs. He had made his peace with death long ago, as antiquaries traditionally used to do. For what season of sunshine there was left, he was more his own master than any younger man can be. And of course he had that special quality that no one young has now, which I suppose comes from having known the security of the world before 1914.

After lunch he took me for a tour of his land. It was nothing more than a small park really, hidden away by hillsides and thin hanging woods. It was hardly more than one twist of valley, a flat bottom widening out towards a shallow river over-shadowed by a tangled tapestry of trees. It looked unlikely ground for an excavation. But as we went he gave a commentary, perfected over years I dare say, that made it sound like the most exciting archaeological site in Britain, and one of the most complex. There were Bronze Age graves up on the hillside, the ramparts and gateway of a fortified camp in the woods, signs of Iron Age activity round the spring, here the find-spot of a Roman coin hoard, there the burial-place of some poverty-stricken Saxon. In north Oxfordshire that is all quite possible, and I had seen some of his finds in the library. But I did sense the presence of a particularly vigorous imagination.

'What do you think?'

'It has everything. All it needs is singing trout like that river in Arcadia.'

'Ah, the singing trout, the famous singing fish. I've written about them. Greek, yes. Just the point. Of course most of this is just rubbish. You'd find the same thing anywhere. There's a hill-fort above Bladon they've used for a water-storage tank. And as for the Anglo-Saxon pottery – horrible, isn't it? Disgusting! But what this place needs is something Greek. Could be, of course. That hill-fort in Somerset – mind how you go over that wire, wretched stuff – that Camelot, they called it, now there they had plenty of Greek pottery and a large Greek church. "Eastern Mediterranean", they called it. Might as well call it bloody Turkish. Hate the Turks. Learnt it from the Serbs. That pottery was as Greek as Greek. That's what we need here, and I'd like to see it before I die. Of course that makes me a tiny bit cautious. The fact is I've found it. That's why I've called you in.'

'Greek A.D.? Christian Greek? Anglo-Saxon period?'

'Well, no. Certainly not. Much better really. Of course you're the one to say. But unless I'm much mistaken this is sixth-century B.C.'

My heart sank. He had hardly a snowflake's chance in a superheated chicken factory of being right. The Greeks got a long way west and a long way north five or six hundred years before Christ, mostly in the way of trade. They were in the hills somewhere south of Paris, near the source of the Seine. Two hundred years later a stray ship or two coasted up north of Wales. If Alexander the Great had lived, his intention was to take over the whole of Western Europe. For all we know to the contrary, he might then have ruled from central Russia to the Atlantic and from India to the polar ice. But as history turned out, you do not expect to find anything Greek on a muddy hillside by the ford of an obscure river in north Oxfordshire. At least nothing so old.

'Are you sure,' I asked Ralph Iggleby, who was breathing heavily now on the slope, 'that these things haven't come here later, in some other way? Could they belong to a Roman villa?'

'We'll see,' he answered. 'We'll see here.'

His excavation was surprisingly neat. It was certainly the remains of a very elaborate grave, plank-built and earth-covered. The mossy-looking bones of a skeleton lay under a plastic sheet just where they must have been found. Everything else had been taken away. It must have been an interesting burial, and it raised countless questions. The experts were not going to like being deprived of their chance to question this earth and these pieces of wood more closely. How many planks had there once been? Was this really a purely timber construction? Was there, among the fragments of wood that survived, any chance of a carbon test to fix the date of the burial?

'Of course,' he observed tranquilly, 'I left him there. Have to call in the coroner otherwise. Lot of trouble and interference. I shall cover all this over. Must keep it from the experts, all those bearded fellows in sandals. Want no trouble from them. Have to do without a carbon test. But I thought you should see it. In confidence of course. I decided over lunch you must be reliable. And I want to know what you think. Most of this is straight Hallstatt: what you might expect. A chamber lined with wood, made of wood really, like a room with no doors or windows. Rotted away long ago of course. Long ago. Rotted away and washed away. Level when I found it. Only got to it because that tree fell. One of my last elms. It survived the disease you know, five years ago was it? I went about injecting them. Then this one went in a storm last year. One of the last elms in Oxfordshire. Coffin-wood, all it's good for now. Well, it can make my coffin. Let's go back.'

In the sixth century B.C. almost nothing is too strange to be true. The soberest text-books record Greek architecture in Spain and in Germany, and Chinese silk and Greek bronze and gold in the burial of some chieftain with a birch-bark cap on the river Neckar. They record a lathe-turned, wooden Greek drinking cup in Bavaria, and a mysterious use of the newest iron wood-working tools from the south in eastern Yorkshire. The material culture associated by its modern discoverers with Hallstatt was wide open to penetration by the Greeks. But in north Oxfordshire, in the middle of an oak forest? The Yorkshire evidence is a wooden boat from the bed of the river Humber. It was made of planks, sawn and adzed and fitted together, and then sewn tight with the long stringy fibres of a yew tree. That hardly constitutes a Greek connection. The question of where the carpenter got his tools is undecided.

Indoors, in the library, the old man showed me what had come out of the grave. There was not much doubt about it. He had some local pottery, badly smashed and not very beautiful, but as far as I could see it was the right age. He had a dented golden bowl like a small soup tureen or a rose-bowl, fresh-looking in the light from the library fire. The decoration round its edge was simple and repetitive; it was surely Hallstatt. So were the weapons. So apparently was a ragged piece of leather in poor condition, that he took to be the ruins of a conical cap. Finally, there were some pieces of Greek painted pottery, most of it from a vessel of great size, but with a lot of pieces missing. And all these treasures he drew from a cupboard in a bronze bowl. A cow stood on each side of the lip of the bowl staring inwards, each cow with a calf climbing up behind it to suckle. If this was Greek animal sculpture it was earlier than the bowl. To judge from the way they were fastened, the cow and calf figures were in fact added later. I thought by their snouts and their awkward legs and their intense innocence, they must be Hallstatt creations, but the bowl was Greek. However the Greeks may at first have used the big bronze bowls that they set on tripods and offered to their gods, maybe this one was used in Germany, or even somewhere in north Oxfordshire, to hold milk.

We both stood a long time in silence, lost in a shadowy world. The silence was broken only when a young girl of a heavenly beauty brought in tea.

2

The reader who has wandered even so far as this into the mazes of my adventure will easily see how at this early stage I was moving rather aimlessly. But it was a paradise where every tree was booby-trapped. The girl who brought in tea was a remote cousin of Ralph Iggleby. She had been to Witney to do the shopping, or else I would have met her at lunch. Nearly every male human being has a certain special type of girl to whom he is vulnerable, and with whom if given a chance he will always make the same mistakes. My downfall has always been just this shimmering kind of girl with a tea-tray, her blue eyes and freckles, her freshness and her comforting severity. I was tugged into her orbit.

I have been married, but I was glad to say goodbye by the time it was over. She took away my comb and kept her place in *Vogue* with it. She lost my socks. She borrowed my tooth-brush to clean out her guinea-pigs. She discovered wine and gave up cooking, and I discovered gin and gave up eating. She was often as drunk as I was, she never went to bed earlier and often got up later. There were faults on both sides of course. I became more priggish and tight-lipped as she went wilder. Gin is a depressing diet. Perhaps we ought to have had a child, but life never looked settled enough. It was a tempestuous eighteen months followed by another awful year of hurt feelings. We were neither of us to start with old enough to look after the other one. What a long time ago it seems. It was in the years just after that catastrophe that I worked hard and continuously to build up a stock of specialized knowledge, the store-room behind the shop-front that every scholar needs. In the end the habit of work became my consolation. The specialized knowledge had soon gone out of date.

This sensational new girl was called Joy; old Ralph Iggleby introduced her as his secretary and his assistant and his right hand. She gave us teacups without moving us away from the treasure.

'Has anyone else seen it?' I asked.

The old man looked a little embarrassed. He fiddled with a pair of massive tortoise-shell spectacles.

'He had a dinner party,' said Joy. 'He couldn't resist.'

'Only the vicar you know, and the local antiquarians. No trouble from them. The vicar and the doctor and so on. They always know about my excavations, you see. Nothing private in the country. I always have shown local people. Same in my father's day. The vicar's most interested I must say, the scholarly kind. Pupil of old Canon Claud. No such canons as that nowadays, and few such vicars as our vicar. Talks about retiring, but I hope he'll see me out. Have you heard him preach? Splendid, dry voice, like a gargoyle. Common prayer services of course. And the doctor, he's safe. Gave me some help as a matter of fact. Over buckthorn. Trickier subject than you'd think. We have it here on the hillside.'

I must have shown I was out of my depth there, as Joy came to my rescue. 'In the *Shrubs and Trees of British Hill-forts*,' she said. It was only then that I realized who Ralph Iggleby was. He had written a thick, deviously learned, unreadable and invaluable book with that title. It must have been published long before my time, in the thirties maybe; it had huge pages and terrible photographs.

'I'd forgotten,' I said, 'about the buckthorn.'

'Powerful purge,' he said. 'Most powerful. They found buckthorn seeds at St Alban's where the monks' lavatories used to be. *Rhamnus cathartica*. Not common on hill-forts. No need for it. Clergy are all the same, Claud Jenkins always said so. George Herbert maintained all country persons ought to plant rhubarb. But you do find alder buckthorn. That's where Doctor Saintly helped. Alder buckthorn's an even worse purge. Oh, awfully powerful. We did experiments. There was an old woman before the war, lived in a cottage here. Nothing but alder buckthorn would move her. Most curious. Dogwood. Makes wonderful charcoal. Crackles up like gunpowder. That's what they used it for of course in the hill-forts. *Frangula alnus*. Not a rhamnus at all. Only called buckthorn because of the purging I dare say. What do you think Jonson? You know my book? Funny name frangula.'

'Now Ralph, Mr Jonson doesn't want to hear about your disgusting insides.'

'Course he does dear. Vicar takes buckthorn, or so I've always believed.'

'The Athenians chewed it one day a year,' I hazarded, 'right through the age of Pericles. To purge themselves of the spirits of their ancestors.'

'Quite right. Quite sensible. Rhamnous is a place in Attica. Hard to get to in my day. Still bits of marbles lying about in the bushes then. And pottery like this.'

'You haven't had it photographed?'

'No fear, no. No photographs. But you can draw it if you like. Drawing's more accurate anyway, and less chance of stray copies. Stray photographs lead to stray visitors.'

'I'd like to draw these pieces if I might. Then I could tell you more about them.'

'Joy, you help him. She helps me you know. Good little drawer.'

So Joy and I sat side by side drawing the bits of Greek pottery, piece by piece. Her drawings were at least as useful as mine, though for her pieces I missed the greatest benefit of copying for myself, which is what you learn in the concentrated process of drawing. In fact I was so distracted that I had to do some of my drawings two and three times over to get them right. Meanwhile my learned host was shuffling through papers. Time flew by with ironical comments from an astronomical long-case clock. I made up my mind then that the things I had to say had better be said to Joy alone, or at least through her, not to the old antiquarian directly. My principal feeling was that to keep these treasures, and heaven knows what else he might have squirrelled away in his library cupboards, was very dangerous indeed.

I had seen no evidence of even the simplest burglar alarm. Yet at least in the village there must be gossip by now. And how many people in Oxford had known? Had he entrusted his secrets to the moated grange expert or to Frowser? Did Ralph Iggleby go to London perhaps, and did he gossip there? What was the legal position? In the nineteenth century the archaeologically minded gentry opened the tops of grave mounds like so many steak and kidney puddings. But the law about ancient treasures was getting stricter every year. Ralph Iggleby appeared to be protected by two heavy-looking swords and an obsolete pistol hanging on his wall. He was lucky to have kept the pistol. If he had ever taken out a fire-arms certificate for it, then the police would have been round to collect it by now; in the last few years the police had confiscated every old weapon in Oxfordshire. No doubt it was a relic of his Serbian days; no doubt he had kept it in happy illegality ever since.

'Fish,' he announced. 'You were mentioning the singing fish in the river Aroanios in Arcadia. They were spotted and they sang like thrushes. A loud whistle around sunset. Old Frazer was told by the peasants in 1895 that they were trout. I wonder in what language? They said the fish chirped like little birds

13

when you netted them. And I see that Jesuit who did the Penguin Pausanias has some other Jesuit with some fish in Ceylon. They make a thin, sour, chirping noise. They would. Not very relevant anyway. I've written about those Arcadian fish. Here's an off-print for you, would you like it? Just so you don't think I never publish now. Have some sherry, shall we? Stay to dinner?'

I accepted the off-print with delight, but declined dinner. I had already stayed a long time too long for lunch, and had hopes of coming back to that library in the near future. It smelt vaguely of cloves and Balkan tobacco; the photographs of mules had faded to match the still more ancient photographs of cricket teams. An old sofa, which must once have been a dog's nestling place, was still half draped in a dog blanket. Ralph Iggleby seemed rather to feel his way about in that room by touch and by memory than to notice what was in it. I said my goodbyes and moved to look for my bicycle. But I was pursued by his voice.

'Bicycle? Did you cycle here? Leave it. Terrible rattling contraptions. Fetch it another day, in the light. Joy will run you back.'

Nothing could have suited me better. The wind had got up, and romantic clouds were flinging themselves across the darker sky. The trees in the park were sighing and tossing like something out of Shakespeare. It was no night for a bicycle.

'What you ought to know about Ralph,' she began as I settled myself into the dark green vintage Bentley, 'is that he's worried. He's nobody's fool, and he's afraid this treasure of his might be some kind of awful, malevolent practical joke. That's why he won't show it off. And why he really needs reassurance.'

'I'd like to give him that. But it hardly can be a joke, can it? Is that gold real gold?'

'Oh yes, he's tested that. Everything is what it looks like, so far as we can test it here. He's even been to the British Museum with just a drawing of something and they confirmed it.'

'They might confirm anything. I knew someone who went there with a Luristan bronze buckle. He was sent to five different departments, and they said it was either a shoehorn or a caviar spoon, modern.'

'Well, it does sound a bit offbeat.'

'Not at all. There's an entire book about them published in Paris in the war. *Les oiseaux éléphantomorphes*. No, it's true.'

'My God, I see how you and Ralph are going to be friends.'

'Oh I don't know. You're more my generation. Or at least I'm halfway.'

'Well, I love whoever loves Ralph. But he's up to something with you. You're a special card he's deliberately playing, and I don't really know why.'

She drove with concentration, and yet I could sense a warmth, even a sprouting affection, in her cheeks and her eyes and her hurried glances.

'Is all that stuff safe?' I asked her. 'Does he want me to advise him to put it in a bank or a museum? Why me?'

'Oh, he's known about you for ages. He's had his eye on you. He knows everyone in Oxford in his own line of enquiry, and he can't stand most of them. But he really favours you. I don't think he wants to be safe, do you? But he doesn't want to be fooled. And of course he's short of money. He might have to sell something.'

'Is he? Oh dear. Him as well.'

'Him more than most. Prehistoric pension, terribly tiny. And a fixed income of course. He puts up wages when he hears anyone else does. He goes on buying books. It does all cost. I think he wants you to do something or say something or discover something that he can't or won't find out himself. I don't know what.'

'Left here. Now steady, round there to the right. That's it. Well it really is frightening. If that stuff is what it looks like, it's worth I don't know what. Half a million or more. And that's sold separately. But taken together it's unique, and terribly important as I suppose you both realize. Now along here, by those trees, there's a turning.'

We were soon home, painfully soon. Joy was unwilling to come in on any excuse, but we promised to see each other soon, and to be in touch about Ralph Iggleby's strange new toys. One question that turned out later to be important I did manage to slip in. He was unmarried, and he had no obvious heir.

'Oh no. He's a famous bachelor. There's a pool where they

swim on the river, with a huge notice, *Men and Boys Only*. But no boyfriends either. Ralph is the happiest natural bachelor I've ever known. I wondered at first if I'd disturb him. Not at all. He treats me like a pet godchild.'

'Thanks for the drive.'

'Bye.'

One short kiss and she was off, and I was indoors, mooning over my mantelpiece museum, my little pieces of antiquity picked up cheap and long ago.

> 'And gaslight touches to a softer gold
> The broken, sorrowful divinities.'

Not quite gaslight, that would be an exaggeration even of my way of life. Though they do speak of bringing North Sea gas to this village, and when they do I shall not only cook with it, I shall light myself to my last long bed with it. Or if it were Joy a new bridal bed with it. Forty years of electricity have been enough. In my grandfather's time, Ralph Iggleby not being the only person with a grandfather, electric light was new. And what a mistake. Here and there in the country you can still hear private electric generators, pounding away like water-rams. But in his day country houses had private gas works. One might ask Ralph Iggleby, I was thinking. We shall see it all again in the next twenty years. And Joy, how ravishing she would be by gaslight.

I picked up the off-print about singing fish. It certainly had a scientific basis. There was the gratitude expressed once again for scientific advice to Doctor Saintly. It was an article published in an extremely distinguished, solidly obscure periodical. It charted the recorded decibels of a whole multitude of singing fish. The whales of course, one had heard them, that plaintive call, hardly a song, certainly not a whistle. The mysterious communications of dolphins and how they loved one another. The tropical toadfish can do one hundred decibels. Something about the maigre, a sort of sea-perch, sciaena. Drummers or croakers underwater can be heard on the sea's surface. Aha! Nearer. Bony-structured fish with swimming bladders make the loudest noises. Unlikely to be trout, however many spots they had. Quite. The swimming bladder of the carp gives it a magnification of one thousand. My goodness. Game, set and match to the old man. Carp of course. I wondered if clever Joy had read it.

The telephone shattered my solitude. Sometimes it purrs, at other times it rages. This time I knew before I picked it up that something was wrong.

'Saintly here. Doctor Saintly.'

'Yes. This is 471. Ben Jonson.'

'Ah, good. I say, I want to talk to you about a patient of mine, an old patient and an old friend. Ralph Iggleby. Did you see him today?'

'Yes, at lunch.'

'How much did he drink?'

'Not much. Is he all right?' I wanted to say, does Joy know? 'Terribly over-excited. High blood-pressure you see. Not the thing at his age. High cholesterol. Arterio-sclerosis. The usual.'

'Is he ill now?'

'Could drop off you know, any moment. Look here, did he consult you about this digging of his? I want you to calm him. Be a wet blanket. If and but, you know. No need to pursue it far.'

'He seemed awfully strong to me. Walked me miles without drooping.'

'Layman's eye, Jonson, if I may say so. Flukes in his eyes. Veins standing out on his legs. A whole history. And he isn't at all young.'

'Well, I'm sorry to hear it, and of course I'll do what I can. I should think Joy is your best ally. What does she say?'

'She won't understand, Jonson, she won't accept it. The old chap's going, but let it be slowly. I want you to put a complete damper on all this. Forget it. He'll forget it himself, you see. I've known him years.'

'Well, doctor, I'm in a difficult position. Let's say if you like that 1 won't refer to it again if he doesn't. But I have to go there, I left a bicycle.'

'Oh damn. But do treat it as I say. Don't go feeding his fancies. Eh? Ah.'

'I think I have to do what I promised. I shall check some

17

drawings I made of Greek pottery, and I shall fetch my bicycle, and beyond that I shall consult Joy. She seemed sensible enough to me.'

He muttered something scarcely polite, and the phone went dead. It left me considerably puzzled. The mystery that hung already over Ralph Iggleby was thickening by the hour. My own loyalties were quite clear. He was my new old friend, and Joy was my new young friend. But even deeper in my heart there lay a loyalty to the things he had found, to sorting what was genuine from what was not, to the truth about what came out of the earth. In the end, it was a loyalty to the things themselves, to their meaning, and their history. My sort of loyalty is hard to defend. But it takes a lot more confidence than I had in Doctor Saintly to shake it.

That night I made some progress with the drawings. After nine I phoned Ralph Iggleby's number. Just as I hoped, it was Joy who answered. Ralph was perfectly well. The doctor had come to dinner. Ralph told him with triumphant glee about how I was going to solve all problems. The doctor had looked a bit bleak, and made a phone call. There was no physical examination of Ralph Iggleby, and no mention of his health. The doctor had left early, having promised to play chess with the vicar. I told her I was off to London next morning, and we agreed to meet in the evening, for dinner at my house. Tomorrow seemed an ordinary day.

3

In north Oxfordshire the weather reports alter quite often, but the weather almost never alters. So it was the usual cold grey morning, the same wind had been blowing since the spring equinox, not quite amounting to a gale; a misty, rough atmosphere had abolished every horizon. It might easily turn to rain at any minute.

All the ordinary reference books are easier to get at in Oxford than they are in London, but the British Museum has a vast collection of Greek painted pottery, and that was what I wanted next. Almost nothing of the greatest paintings of the Greeks has survived. But virtually every Athenian painter who ever decorated vases in the classical centuries has been identified and catalogued. The vase-paintings happen to survive only because pottery is hard to destroy and impossible to melt down and reuse. Sorting all that out was substantially the work of one generation, and within that generation of one man. When I was young we were so over-awed by that achievement, and by the old man himself, his sweet old-fashioned touches of elegance, his depth and range and his face like a tragic mask, that the subject itself had a disproportionate prestige.

The game he taught us to play, among the appalling debris of thousands and thousands of pieces of broken pottery, was one that none of us forgot. He could spot that a fragment he had seen thirty years ago in Naples belonged to the same pot as two pieces in a London shop, and remember that a bit of the rim was in a particular cupboard in the Vatican. He would sometimes employ months or years of diplomacy to bring all the pieces together, and he was reported after some particularly mind-boggling success to have drunk champagne in Oxford out of the mended cup, broken two and a half thousand years ago and its pieces scattered on a Calabrian mountainside. Nowadays the dew had withered from the wild roses. One had simply to look up the painter in the published lists. Ralph Iggleby clearly had some nice bits and pieces of a cup from the twenties of the sixth century B.C. I reckoned it was by someone called the Dolphin Painter.

The Dolphin Painter was not the highest class of artist. At a time when single clear figures, beautifully drawn, were coming into fashion, and when a new subtlety in the disposition of space had appeared and already announced the fine art of the coming century, the Dolphin Painter disliked to see spaces unoccupied. He had the habit, unique in his or, so far as I know, in any generation of Greek vase-painters, of doodling dolphins in the background. In some of his works the dolphins were big and handsome, in others they were perfunctory. In some cases you could argue they offered a topographic hint, in a few perhaps a touch of religious enthusiasm. But taken all in all, there were too many of these dophins for any logical explanation. They appeared in mid-air, and they sported between pillars. There was no mistaking him. I was fond of the Dolphin Painter. A lot of his work had turned up at Naukratis, at an early Greek merchant settlement in Egypt with its own Greek sanctuaries and its own special wonders. Most of that material was in the British Museum, and I thought I owed it to Ralph Iggleby to check the detail of the drawings I had against the Museum's examples. There was no reason to suppose the Dolphin Painter ever lived at Naukratis. Even if, as I then thought, the Naukratis vases represented eighty per cent or more of his surviving work, it might all have come from a single shipping. If in fact he was in the habit of drawing his dolphins for export, then Ralph Iggleby's Hallstatt grave with dolphin pottery in north Oxfordshire acquired a faint shadow of plausibility. A wrecked ship, driven off course and washed up somewhere? I was extremely reluctant to allow a Greek ship trading so far north, because all the French evidence suggested overland penetration northwards from Marseilles. But there was no reason why Mont Lassois, where Greek material was abundant, should not have traded north. An exchange of princely gifts? An off-shoot of the amber trade with the Baltic? A dynastic marriage with Heuneberg? My mind as usual was painfully open.

Not everything from Naukratis in the British Museum is on display. So while I was arranging to get into the cellars, not nearly as difficult as it sounds if you know what you want, I swapped gossip with John Gresham, a friend who got stuck in the Greek and Roman Department, halfway up the ladder of promotion for ancient art historians, many years ago, and has been there ever since. I find him a purist, but a generous-minded one, and if you are not intimidated by his thick, almost rimless spectacles, and his ancient, respectable suit, which I have never known him change, he is easy to deal with. He was scornful of my dolphins.

'More of those nasty things?'

'You do have a lot already I suppose.'

'Mm. We do. Hundreds of awful little bits. You're not going to write about him are you?' This much more hopefully. 'Clear him out of the way?'

'Not quite that. I just wanted to check these pieces.'

'Where did they come from? Naukratis?'

'Not directly. An old chap asked me about them.'

'Oh. That's a nice one, there, I suppose, in its awful way. Probably Naukratis.'

'I don't think so.'

'Oh, there's a lot from Naukratis wandering around you know. Mm. Might even have passed through here. Or bought in Cairo? Mm. I was thinking about this foul painter the other day. Why? I can't remember why. If you are writing anything I did have an idea. Don't suppose it would work.'

'Try me.'

'Well, the dolphins between the pillars. On a big pot we have on display. You must know it.'

'Yes, of course I do. I think it's the one he was named after, isn't it? I've just looked at it.'

'What about the Siwa Oasis?'

'I'm afraid I'm lost.'

'Mm. Sorry. The city of Cyrene had close relations in the sixth century with the god of the Siwa Oasis. Zeus Ammon. When the other Greeks got there later they found it was full of dedications from Cyrene. Dolphins on pillars. Mm? No?'

'No,' I said firmly. 'No.'

'Oh well, worth a try. Mm. No. I suppose you're right. Oh I remember now. Yes, what brought it to mind. It might interest you. There was someone in here before Christmas trying to sell us more of the stuff. Rather like yours, come to think of it. Bought in Cairo I suppose. So now it's cropping up in Oxford, is it? Same source I dare say.'

'Do you happen to remember who he was?'

'Well we do usually keep a note of that even if we don't buy. Now who was it? A dealer, I'm sure, a London dealer. I could find out. Why don't you look in when you've finished downstairs?'

'Could you really look it up for me? It so happens it might be very useful. He might even have the rest of the cup.'

'I doubt that. But yes, I will. We might go to lunch if you finish in time?'

'Oh, I think if you can do that for me I might take you out to quite a good lunch.'

'Ah,' he rubbed his hands and he polished his glasses. 'Not the club then.'

'Certainly not the club.'

We belong to the same club. It has an uninhabited library where many a quiet plot has been plotted. It has also a huge, sepulchral coffee room with vast, sepulchral portraits and a famous, sepulchral view, the sort of room that station hotels used to have. In the good old days one hated such rooms, and such clubs and such hotels, but now that there are so few left in the world I find a morose comfort in them. Indeed, nostalgia has so eaten away my resistance that when I found a three-piece dining-room string band in a hotel at Belgrade just as there used to be at Paddington, I sat enthralled for night after night, only last year. Still, the coffee at our club is served from a leaking urn, and the food tends to be the same pie as last week and perhaps last season. And for a celebration, our club produces very old, rather flat, urine-coloured champagne, a great luxury to sophisticated palates but not to me. So not the club.

There is something mildly surrealist about the cellars of the British Museum. So many marble heads without noses. So many lumpish pieces of antique, provincial art. Then the packing cases with the names of famous expeditions. And the endless desert of fragments laid out on trays. An hour or two down there more than satisfied my curiosity. I even began to share John Gresham's despair about the Dolphin Painter, as if it was somehow the artist's fault that his vases broke into so many small bits. Of course, since the substance of pottery is nearly indestructible, if Naukratis were completely excavated we ought to recover every last fragment of every single vase. But pottery can crumble to a kind of sand. And nothing has ever been perfectly excavated.

John Gresham came beaming out of his lair to lunch, with his glasses freshly polished and his suit more venerable-looking than ever. He even had a hat, which I thought dashing in an official of the Museum. We went to eat in a Greek restaurant of which there were good reports. It was already busy, but we were early and found a table, and the London prices for the best Greek cooking, so long as the restaurant is fairly new, are still not so high as French prices. The salad was perfect, with olives like young plums and salt like a heavy frost. The taramas was in season, or at least the taramasalata was not that cement-like frozen mix which lies in heavy, bland puddles on the plates of most restaurants nowadays, and disgraces the colour pink. All the ingredients of lunch were wonderful, in fact they were exactly what a Greek restaurant meal would be like in Greece if the customers there could afford those ingredients. This place even served Beaujolais Villages, which in Athens, as in Oxford, you would be lucky to find unless lunch was thirty pounds a head.

The reader will have to forgive my dwelling rather lovingly on that lunch. I have concentrated on the food and drink not only because we both did at the time, but also because the gossip of old friends and fellow students is not interesting to outsiders. And above all because it was the last moment of sanity and tranquillity in that long adventure. Looking back to that moment now, I see that things had already gone too far. It was no longer possible to avoid the consequences of decisions already taken. I was due to step out of the world in which it is an act of daring to go to lunch at a Greek restaurant, to step right outside it. Perhaps decisions may be the wrong word. Things were already much more entangled than I understood.

John Gresham gave me the name of a dealer in antiquities who ran a shop somewhere off Oxford Street. He was an Armenian with Egyptian connections, and his name was Touloupian, but the shop was called Bowen's. So the next move was simple. I called on him about three in the afternoon. His shop-front contained most of a broken Egyptian mummy-case and a pair of stuffed crocodiles. The museum in Oxford has two hundred of those, and who knows whether they may not be stuffed with papyrus? With the lost plays of Aristophanes? You never know in my trade. But I was betting against it. And for years I have defended my peace of mind with a strong prejudice against the vast flood tide of late Egyptian art. Still, the connections with Egypt did helpfully suggest Naukratis.

The interior of the shop was dim and smelt of its deep carpets. The antiquities were in glass cases, brightly lighted round the walls, and the only other light glittered discreetly over a desk. Yes, of course I might look around. Had I any special interest? Later perhaps. The display of Greek things was not very grand. The Roman glass was of better quality. One archaic terracotta had been worn away by time and the action of water to a simple and marvellous shape, as if it was by Henry Moore. Someone was going to pay through the nose for that freak of chance. On a bottom shelf stood one of those late, crudely executed, robustly imagined pots from the Greek settlements in southern Italy, that stand on the top of bookshelves in Harley Street and Eaton Square. Not a trace of the Dolphin Painter.

'I wondered if I might see Mr Touloupian?'

The girl at the desk bestirred herself from some intimate reverie.

'Of course,' she said. 'I'll just see if he's engaged. What was it about?'

'Some Greek pottery I'm trying to trace. To match it really. It's by someone called the Dolphin Painter.'

'Yes, of course, sir. What name shall I say?'

'He won't know my name, but John Gresham sent me along. My name is Jonson.'

'Mm.' She buzzed a low-toned buzzer. 'Dr Jonson, to see Dr Touloupian, about some Greek pottery. Right.'

Touloupian entered like a suaver version of the Demon King, up a noiseless staircase through a hole in the floor among the shadows. His manners were excessively correct, his head was handsome, his fingers were long and supple. Perhaps he kept them so like an ancient Chinese mandarin, by manipulating walnuts with his fingertips. He certainly seemed Chinese, in a more essential respect; he looked as if he lived by the pre-Confucian proverb 'Eat soft and spit hard'. I believe in eating hard when I have to, but I am a soft spitter. Touloupian terrified me. His eyes were as hard as stones.

'We do handle such pieces from time to time. I have always thought, haven't you, that the Dolphin Painter is under-estimated. Those who have the privilege to work in museums are rather spoilt, don't you think? So many wonderful things. One can become jaded.'

I agreed one could become jaded. Touloupian took comfort from the ring on his finger, or was it from the polish on his shoes?

'Of course, if we can help you to trace something, we should be delighted. Is it a piece you are trying to buy?'

'Under certain circumstances, if I could afford it, I suppose I might. But it's more a question of where some pieces have come from.'

'Ah.' That flexible monosyllable expressed a great deal. There was going to be little chance of eating me softly, he seemed to think. So he was going to spit me out hard.

'Are these pieces you own?'

'It's only that they might have been bought here. It was an incomplete cup, and you might even know where to find the rest of it.'

'Exactly. I see. That does happen I admit. We would never split up pieces of one cup, of course not. But you think we might have found more fragments later. That is possible. Every dealer has a big box of fragments and it isn't always the dealer that first matches them. Even at Sotheby's, ten or fifteen years ago when all our hearts were lighter and some of our pockets were heavier. Even there, I went to bid for a box of fragments, and just ten minutes before the sale one of the staff spotted that among them lay almost all the pieces of a very nice cup indeed. I lost it of course. You were thinking of something like that?'

'I hoped you might recognize drawings of the fragments that interest me.'

'Drawings? You have drawings?' His voice sharpened. 'But no photographs? No doubt they are still to be taken. Ah, fine drawings. May I congratulate you, Mr – er – ah, Dr Jonson, of course. On your very fine drawings. Katya, will you go round to the coffee-bar and bring us back coffee? You will take coffee? This calls for a few moments of study.'

Touloupian dealt out the drawings like a man playing patience against the clock. The shop door tinkled. The Roman glass glittered. It was very silent. Touloupian reshuffled the drawings.

'Was it John Gresham who connected these fragments with me?'

'Not with any certainty. He thought you might know the source. They could easily come from Alexandria, or from Cairo.'

'I see, yes, so they could. The Dolphin Painter, I think; no doubt about him. I doubt, you know, whether all his pieces have ever been published. And it might be hard to tell one piece from another. At Tocra, if I remember rightly, they found more vases by the Polos Painter in one ditch than his whole existing works down to that time. And all much the same you know. These things do happen. These pieces might have been found anywhere.'

'There was something strange about them,' I said.

'Oh, genuine enough, I think, don't you? Of course I haven't seen the originals, only these uncanny drawings. It's interesting to me you should connect me with this painter. Rather a compliment. But rare; I rarely see such work as this. My bread and butter is more humdrum. And in the state of the market now. And the state of the Middle East. Who knows? Now you see that terracotta over there?'

I am not perfectly clear what happened next. I turned towards one of the showcases, Touloupian seemed to follow me, and I thought the door-bell tinkled again. Did it, or was that another noise? There was a smash of glass and all the lights went out. Touloupian cursed with the full weight of Eton and Cambridge behind his voice. The darkness seemed full of movement. I edged away into a corner. Someone cannoned into me like a rugby forward. I flung out my arms and found nothing, and with no thought or feeling except for sharp personal fear and somehow shame, I fell headlong downstairs. I remember falling, but then I lost consciousness.

Did something hit me as I fell, after I fell? I am not as young as I was, and I admit I was terribly shaken. I just do not remember how I fell. I know the stairs had no guard-rail, but I have no way of guessing what happened in that room. When I came round I was laid out on a sofa in the gallery downstairs, with a cold compress on my head and my collar loosened. The lights were on. The girl Katya was fluttering with the coffee.

Touloupian was telephoning upstairs. As far as I can be certain, what I first heard was this.

'Get rid of it then. Yes, tonight. This is a disaster. No, I can't help that. No, it alters nothing. No, but what if it turns up? Better be safe. Yes I have those. No, of course not. I promise you there's no damage done. Just do as I say.'

I opened my ageing eyes and groaned with a solemnity that was all too genuine. The phone clicked, and Touloupian came racing downstairs.

'My poor chap, how are you? What happened to you?'

'What happened to anyone? What was it?'

I sat up slowly, and found to my relief I had nothing worse than a headache.

'Give the poor man some coffee.'

I held out a feeble hand for it.

'It was a raid of some kind. A theft. Smash and grab. God knows how they got in. Or how they found the lights.'

'Did they get away with anything?'

'Nothing important. The breakages are the worst. And whatever happened to you. How do you feel?'

'Not too bad, considering.'

'What do you want to do? Can I drive you somewhere? We shall have the police in later. And the insurance people I suppose. Still, you don't seem in any condition to go through that.'

'I didn't really see anything.'

'No, exactly. Shall I find you a doctor?'

'Oh, I don't think so. I think I'm all right. I think I shall just go home to Oxford.'

'Then let me get you a taxi. Katya will see you to the train.'

'Oh there's no need. You need Katya here. The coffee was wonderful.'

'Some more coffee then?'

'No, I'll just go. What a dangerous life you lead.'

This was said as a feeble attempt at a joke, but it nettled Touloupian.

'Dangerous? I should think it is dangerous. So is everyone's life in London. In this street a burglar alarm can blaze away all day like a symphony orchestra and no one pays any attention.

27

This isn't organized crime, this is casual. Because the street isn't safe I have bullet-proof glass in my windows. So what do they do? Enter my premises, fuse my lights, assault my clients and smash a glass bowl that was two thousand years old. And if the police found them what would happen? The mercy of the court. Six months at the longest. A holiday. Damages? They could pay none.'

I had some sympathy with that point of view, but victimized as I felt, I hardly thought it was a hanging offence. Anyway I was concentrating my groggy wits on getting away. Into the open air. Away.

It was only when the train had rolled out of Paddington and I was slumped in a first-class carriage that I realized I had lost the drawings. And there was something about Touloupian's phone call that worried me worse still. The first words I was conscious of. They sounded like 'Listen faintly'. Could they have been 'Listen Saintly'?

4

That night I had dinner with Joy. She was a Lucian Freud girl or a Peter Lanyon girl. Peter Lanyon painted the Cornish landscape from a glider, with the colours swirling round and round like water in a glass. He also drew, in something of the same spirit, a girl's face entitled 'Right Eye 1960'. Joy was that kind of girl. She was also practical I was glad to observe. When I told her I felt too shaky to cook and offered to take her out, she was into my kitchen at once making approving noises about the oranges and the tarragon vinegar, and she was out in my garden plundering the apple mint and the young lettuces. The dinner she produced was sharp, light and memorable, and in our village you can buy champagne in the village pub.

We talked about everything on earth. We told stories about our childhoods and compared notes on foreign cities and the architecture of the Isle of Wight. Funny how we both knew the Isle of Wight. I could feel the creaking of those wicker-work armchairs on the lawn. I could recollect the flashing of the spray round the great wheel of the paddle steamer before the war. She remembered the violets and the orchids on Tennyson Down, and the particular smell of the wind in summer on that warm turf. We talked about the taste of fresh herrings, grilled in the early morning or fried very slowly in almost no fat at all. The conversation turned to mackerel cooked with gooseberries. The word gooseberry is older than it looks. It might come from the Norman French or Frankish or something, but French words for berries are a mystery to me. They seem to have no word now for gooseberry except *groseille à maquereau*.

'Do you know there are wild gooseberries in the woods at Stonehouses?'

'Really wild? Or gone wild? They might be seeds from bird-droppings.'

'Really wild I mean. That's why it's such an old word. Wild gooseberries must be native since before the Normans. The children from the village come picking them every year. Wild gooseberries, wild strawberries, cowslip wine. It's one vast kitchen.'

'They can't be common nowadays?'

'Don't you believe?'

The days were drawing out, but by this time it was a bright moonlit night, and I seized my opportunity.

'Yes I do. But I'd like to see them. Do you feel like the walk?'

'What about you after your bump?'

'Much better for the food and drink, let alone the peace and quiet. A walk is just what I do feel like.'

'All right then.'

'Besides ...'

'Besides what?'

'I'd really like to see the place again, where Ralph dug those things up.'

'In the dark?'

'Well, I'd like to poke about a bit without him being there. We could take a torch. I don't see any other way of doing it

29

without risking offending him.'

'You're right about that. I think he expected you to do something like this. It's as if he was testing something, something he suspected and wanted you to find out.'

'Or to prove no one could find it out.'

'Or that.'

Her face clouded with trouble. She leaned back from the firelight and ran a hand through her hair.

'Was it really a coincidence at Touloupian's shop?'

'How could it not be? What did anyone gain? That Roman glass that was smashed really was beautiful and expensive. Insured I suppose, but as I read Mr Touloupian, he wouldn't destroy a thing like that. No one else knew I was there, except John Gresham. Unless ...'

I felt a coldness in the stomach.

'Unless someone knew that what I was after really was in that shop. They might easily know I went to London. What would they do? Watch that shop, or try to get there first.'

'Suppose they were already in the shop. In some inner lair. Say in his office.'

'That would,' I agreed reluctantly, 'explain almost everything. What I don't know now is whether the door opened again. I just can't remember, and when I try, I get a splitting headache.'

'What you need is early to bed.'

'No, I wouldn't sleep. I really would like to walk. And we really must work this out. We mustn't build too much on guesses. Time seems to be important, though I don't quite see why. Maybe someone's in a panic. I wish I remembered better about the door, and about the phone call.'

'I don't like it for Ralph.'

'Nor do I. It might be imagination, but I fear it. I fear that doctor. And I wonder if we shall ever see those drawings again.'

'Why should they panic so badly, if it's only a malevolent joke?'

'It sounds worse than that, doesn't it? And even as a hoax it would do terrible damage. Ralph would be terribly angry, and he wouldn't be the only one.'

'Let's face it. You're sure in your heart there was no

coincidence. Someone attacked you, and you might have been killed.'

'Thank God I wasn't. Thick skull I suppose, like an elephant.'

'My poor old elephant.'

'The worst part of it was being called "My poor chap" by Touloupian.'

'But you don't mind me?'

'Mind? I love it. In some other world, I'd like to be an elephant.'

'Elephants never forget.'

'And they go for walks in the moonlight. Your poor old elephant.' I put out a hand for hers.

'Amorous elephant. "L'éléphant et l'amour", do you know that story?' But she took my hand and stroked it.

'And a worse one. There was a famous Greek elephant in the market at Alexandria, that fell in love with a market girl. It used to steal apples and pop them down her dress, so that it could feel her breasts.'

'Forward elephant.'

'Your poor elephant.'

'We'd better go and look for these gooseberries while the moon lasts. How shall we go? In the car first?'

'You take the car and I'll take my bicycle. Then I can get home again.'

'I'll drive slowly like a procession.'

'And coronations rise on every green.'

'What?'

'Poem by Pope, to that girl he was in love with. Miss Blount.'

'Love-struck dwarf. Love-struck elephant.'

'Mm.'

So we set off like that. It was not far to Stonehouses. The moonlight was very bright, but the trees huddled together in dark groups and wisps of white ground-mist hung here and there in the field. I hoped it was not going to end as a foggy night. What runs through my mind on nights like that is a sentence of sinister mystery from *Great Expectations*, first read in adolescence, when I first took to walking at night. 'The mist was up on the marshes.' Those few words used to make my spine tingle then, rambling about alone and out of bounds on night-time escapades, and they have not lost all their magic. Spring nights of moonlight are no time for lovers to be out of their beds, or out of one another's arms. 'Will she? Won't she?' I wondered, as I rattled along at my best speed behind the car.

Joy left the car in its garage, but I wheeled the bicycle along beside me, far into the park. In that dark light, with mist gathering in the hollows and under the swimming lime trees, the park seemed much older than the house. The house slumbered like a dog with its chin on its paws. The park was raw, and cold, and ancient. Joy seemed to know her way blindfold, but we took an easier route than the walk with Ralph Iggleby. At first we crunched on gravel paths, then we plunged along a winding turf path between bushes.

Voices. We heard voices. At first we froze. I left the bicycle there, and we put our arms round each other. I shone the torch and we went forward. We must have been close to the fallen tree and the grave. Twigs crackled, and voices sounded again at the edge of the wood, one of them a high-pitched droning upper-class voice I had never heard before. The other was a familiar corncrake voice.

'It's Dr Stoup,' said Joy. 'It's our vicar.'

'And the other one, I do believe, is Frowser.'

'The man who came to tea. What can they be up to?'

'The same as us, I shouldn't wonder. Shall we wait and watch?'

'We'd see nothing from here. No, let's go on.'

We arrived at the boundary of the wood almost together. They were at least as surprised as we had been.

'Good evening vicar,' said Joy.

'Good evening Frowser,' said I.

Frowser grunted.

'Ah, so,' said the vicar, blinking in the torchlight like the White Rabbit. 'Ah so. Well met by moonlight.'

'At your studies Frowser? Metaphor and sentiment? It's a night for it.'

It is not that easy to get under Frowser's guard. He returned my volley easily with a dead-pan expression.

'Study is like the heaven's glorious sun, that will not be

deep-searched with saucy looks.'

Game point to Frowser, I had to admit.

'We have been viewing the woods. Remarkable, in this unearthly moonlight,' intoned Dr Stoup.

'And the excavation?' I asked.

'And our dear friend's excavation. A sad patch of mud, I'm afraid. A most distressing skeleton. And a beautiful tree lost. An elm, you know. One of few. I like to think of them as part of my congregation. Sometimes I fear the chief part. The last few elms. So.'

'It is,' observed Joy guardedly, 'an intoxicating night for a walk.'

'An innocent intoxication,' murmured Dr Stoup. '*Sobria ebrietas, ebria sobrietas.*'

'Humph,' grunted Frowser. 'Can't say that the moonlight sleeps upon this bank. Too much mist. It's a cold night and my feet are wet.'

They were also muddy. So, more interestingly, were his hands. We bade them a ceremonious goodnight, and waited while their torchlight dwindled away towards the village before we in our turn climbed in among the trees.

There was no doubt what they had been doing in the wood. The earth of the excavation had been resifted and combed. If there was anything there to be found that Ralph Iggleby had overlooked, then Frowser and the vicar had found it. They must have gone carefully to work, and the work must have taken them hours. Except for the freshly trampled ground, there was no more trace of their operations than any shower of rain would have obliterated. And what if Ralph Iggleby's finds were genuine? Surely the vicar, surely even Frowser had a right to be interested. It was unjust to accuse them of tomb-robbing, when there was probably nothing left to rob. Or of tampering with an excavation when the excavation had already taken place. Maybe the vicar's curiosity was like mine. There was a good deal to be curious about.

My head was beginning to drift towards sleep, but for what felt like an hour or more I sat on a damp log with Joy and tried to talk all this through. She was much more suspicious of the vicar than I was.

'Dr Stoup is a very strange figure. He used to be a chaplain in some grand school. He had to leave I think, in a hurry. He was lucky not to be unfrocked, or so Ralph says. Ralph got him this job here; the living used to be in his gift. Ralph liked him because he was an antiquarian, an intelligent audience, someone to have to dinner. But I don't think Ralph has ever really trusted him.'

'But what can he want, at his age? He must be near retirement.'

'He is. He's retiring to our childhood paradise, to the Isle of Wight. I don't know what he wants.'

'Has he got a house there, or relations?' I asked idly.

'No, I don't think so. The word is, he's building a ghastly little bungalow.'

'Well then, he may want money.'

'That's another mystery. Dr Stoup has always seemed to have money. Not much, but more than a vicar would have. He buys books, and he drinks burgundy and claret from Berry Brothers in London. That must be expensive.'

'It always was only just possible. Now the prices are over the moon. Touloupian certainly wants money... What about Doctor Saintly? Is he rich?'

'Like the vicar. Very well off for a country doctor. But with things as they are, almost everyone we know is desperate for money, even Ralph.'

'And if this hoax, supposing it is a hoax, is some kind of conspiracy, which I think it would have to be, can you be one hundred per cent certain that old Ralph Iggleby is the victim and not one of the conspirators?'

'I would have sworn that. What impression did you have?'

'The same. But I had to ask you.'

'Indeed you did. The trouble is one can never be what you called one hundred per cent certain what goes on in his old head. But I lived through the time when he found these things, and I saw how amazed, really how thrilled and almost shaken he was, and then the weeks and weeks of looking up books and sending for photographs and seeing if it was all possible. That wasn't acting. And you know it is just possible.'

'Oh yes, it is just possible. What they call the Hallstatt culture was in touch with the Mediterranean. Not only Greek things turn up in the wilds of Germany, but local imitations of Greek things. There are certain kinds of bronze vessels that first came to Europe through Greece or from further east, and very soon there were local substitutes travelling down from the north west. It isn't impossible for one rich farmer, or a rich king of farmers, in the middle of Oxfordshire in the sixth century B.C., to have owned everything that was found in that grave. It's just a staggering coincidence. The private excavation, the secrecy, and no carbon date even though it was a wooden tomb. And then if you were going to plant some nice, datable Greek pottery in a phoney excavation, fragments anyone could pick up in Cairo or Alexandria are just what you might use. And then there's the mystery of Dr Saintly. And Touloupian's shop. And now the vicar and Frowser.'

'What were they looking for?'

'The rest of that cup. No rich burial like this would have only fragments of a cup. That's more like the Yongy Bongy Bo.'

'One old jug without a handle
Two old chairs and half a table
These were all the worldly goods
In the middle of the woods
Of the Yongy Bongy Bo.'

'Exactly. If there were really only those fragments, this is a hoax. And where actually are the other bits? Either somewhere in this wood, or somewhere in Touloupian's shop, or in Egypt. Unless that bloody vicar took them.'

'Have we any other clue at all?'

'Oh, I don't know. Let's go and look for gooseberry bushes.'

'It's as well we didn't have to convince the vicar that that was why we were here.'

We wandered away along the edge of the woods until we could hear the river. The moonlight gleamed on everything that showed, but the ground-mist was thicker near the water. We were walking waist-deep in it. That was a drowsy, wandering walk, and I am not sure how soon we turned back towards the house. It was true about the gooseberries, but they looked like any other bushes in the dark. It was soon after we turned, at about one in the morning, that I saw lights among the dark, distant windows of the house. Nothing strange about that, but was there not another light, a torch or a lamp of some kind, moving about outside?

Ground-mist plays tricks on the eyesight. When the moon strikes it and you look down on it from a mountainside, it can seem like a bright black expanse of water illuminated by the moon's beams. I could not make out with any certainty whether the distant lamp was a reflection from inside the house, or truly a wandering light in the park. Nor could Joy be certain. We began to hasten, and as we did so the mist increased. It came from nowhere, every whisper of breeze added to it. It was still thin and vaguely fuming, still really a ground-mist, but now it began to muffle the woods and the moon began to be hidden behind scarves of racing vapour.

It was darker and we had to pick our way. Fortunately Joy knew the place blindfold, and we made straight for the house. The moving light was swallowed up in billowing mist. I began to cough, and Joy began to shiver. We were quite close under the walls of the house before we could make them out. They were black in the dark and mist, and sweating with moisture. There was a lighted ground-floor room somewhere away to the right. I turned to ask Joy what room it was. At that moment there came a bang, the shot of a gun. A noise of shattering glass. Then a terrible cry. It was terribly loud, terribly painful, in every way terrible. It was a shocking sound.

We ran for the door, but somewhere else in the darkness another door slammed. Running footsteps echoed away into the park. There was no other sound at all.

5

At those dreadful moments things seem to move in slow motion. Some kind of emergency self awakes and takes over. It was clear to me at once, since I must speak of my own experience not of Joy's, that nothing would be gained by rushing out in pursuit of the footsteps, whatever they meant. The mist had won its campaign against the moonlight, and marshalled its insubstantial armies all round us. Whiteness had already swallowed up the fugitive. It was also clear enough that I had just heard murder committed, if such a crime existed in the world. That cry could have meant nothing else. I had never in my life heard such rage and sadness.

Beyond all this, my first concern was Joy. She was running to the door with tottering feet, and I trembled to think what she might find inside it. Of course I must go with her, look after her, take over if possible. She obviously believed she could help. I doubted that. My blood had already run cold, and I caught at her arm as we ran.

'Not so fast. Let me go first.'

'It's Ralph! It's Ralph! Didn't you hear? We must help him.'

'Please let me go first.'

'No, we'll both go. Quickly. Through here. He's ... Oh God. Oh Ralph.'

He lay half across the great library table he used for a desk. The pistol was still smoking. It lay by his hand. But no pistol had killed him. He was a very ugly sight indeed. Joy crumpled up in a chair and covered her face, and I came very close to vomiting. Someone had taken one of those awful cavalry sabres, sharp enough and heavy enough for any kind of butchery, human or animal, and smashed in his head with it. The sword was gone from its place. Thank God we had not gone blundering out in pursuit, into that mist.

There was no human help to be given. I led Joy out of the reeking room and asked her where I should take her.

'There's a morning room,' she said, 'down here.' As we went into it a woman in a dressing-gown appeared at the head of the stairs.

'Oh Miss Joy,' she said. 'That awful noise. Is Mr Iggleby all right? He's not in his bed.'

'No Mary,' said Joy, 'it isn't all right. You'd better come down and sit with us. We shall have to telephone for the police. We've had a burglary and I'm afraid poor Mr Iggleby ... Now Mary, come in here and we'll make a fire. Poor Mr Iggleby is dead, Mary.'

'Oh I knew it from that noise. Was he shot with a gun, miss?'

'Something like that. I don't want you to go into the library until the police come.'

'Oh miss, and him so kind and old. It's like the way they go attacking the pensioners nowadays. Nobody's safe, miss. I'd hang them, the wicked scum, beg your pardon, miss.'

'So would I, Mary. So would I dear. Where are the matches?'

I had some matches and the fire flared up restfully. I offered to Joy to go and telephone.

'Oh yes of course. But no. The phone's in the library. It's the only one.'

I was not reluctant to go back into the library alone. For one thing, I was still not quite sure how the events that surrounded his death had taken place, and it ought to be easy to observe that. Secondly, I needed, I badly needed to know what, if anything, had been taken. I would have to talk to the police about that.

The old man had been hit right on the top of his head. Where the top of his head had been. The pistol had blown out a pane of glass, just in front of him. It had been fired only once, we heard that much. His cry had come later, as he died or saw that he was going to die. He had been sitting at his desk facing that window, and fired his gun once, and then died. He could not have turned away and stood up to get the pistol, so it was loaded beside him with the safety catch off. Did those cumbersome old weapons have safety catches? Yes, there it was. And whoever hit him, with the sword or something like it, already had that down from the wall as well.

Almost like a duel. No, that was impossible. But if it was the sword that was used, and something told me it was, then whoever handled it was a familiar friend. Not a burglar in a mask, but someone to whom Ralph Iggleby would show it, a fellow veteran or a fellow antiquary. And why would he do such a thing or how would this friend get him to do it? Because there sat Ralph Iggleby in his library, after one in the morning, with the pistol from the same wall on the table beside him. So they made a joke of it. Ralph Iggleby took down the sword to turn the conversation off why he had the pistol down already.

Then he feared something, or somebody, already. But not this familiar friend? At least, not while he had a pistol beside him which he knew was loaded and ready to fire. Nor did he think of the sabre as a weapon. Or not until too late. He was outwitted in fact. He fired his pistol only once, and inaccurately and too late, poor old soldier. And then that cry of rage and despair, as the sword came down. Not even the time to dodge, or to put an arm up. An old man not able to move fast enough from his chair. He had relied utterly on the pistol, and the rage and despair were about missing, losing, being outwitted. If that was true, then maybe after all he did suspect this familiar friend from the beginning. Maybe it was a battle of wits between old chess partners. Perhaps literally so. These thoughts passed through my mind during the time it took to smoke a cigarette, which also abated the foul smell of blood and the sweetish pungent smell of smoke that lingered in the room. It was not a nice two or three minutes. And I was terribly grieved for the old man.

I took the phone to dial, but it was dead. I tried again. Quite dead. I traced the wire to its worm-hole in the wall, but the wire was intact. The telephone wire must have been snipped outside the house. Somewhere outside in the mist that lay close up against the windows. When? Had this meeting been planned as murder? Surely planned, at least because Ralph Iggleby had sat there waiting for it, and he had known this night was dangerous. Waiting for it, but not sure enough of himself to confront his old chess partner. Not quite sure enough. But the other one knew. He was as bold as he was cool. It was only then that I began to wonder whether I was being watched. Whether the house was being watched. Whether the night's horrors were over.

Was robbery involved at all, or was the whole quarrel a battle of wits, a kind of blackmail? My feeling was that robbery was going to turn out to be secondary. What I expected to find missing were the fragments of Greek pottery, the work of the Dolphin Painter. They were apparently the vulnerable point of this whole enterprise. They were also the only thing I might know more about, and find out quicker about, than Ralph Iggleby. He had guessed there was something wrong, either because the identification and the date were simply too easy, or because part of the cup was missing. He had wanted me to track something down, to nail it. Well, I would try and do just that for him. This was going to be team chess, and I was on his side.

Meanwhile it ought to be easy to establish what, if anything, had been taken. The library cupboards were not locked. I remembered what lived where. And there, sure enough, were the contents of the grave, except of course for the uncovered skeleton out in that mist, and except, as I had foreseen, for the fragments by the Dolphin Painter. Something tapped against a window-pane, surely some finger or tendril of a plant. But I jumped, and I found myself shuddering. I had no intention of going outside before morning, or letting anyone else go. I recocked the pistol, put the safety catch on, and carried it with me out of the room.

Joy or Mary had made some tea. It was just what we needed, hot, strong, and sweet, as used to be recommended in first-aid books. Now they say give nothing and move nobody, but I know what world I would sooner live in. I made no secret of having the pistol, which set Mary's face into a grimmer expression and turned Joy paler.

'In case anyone's loitering about,' I said. 'In case they come back. I shall sit up, and in the morning we can get the police.'

'Hang 'em I would,' said Mary. 'But shooting'll do for a start. Mind you shoot to kill.'

'Don't you worry. I shall sit on the stairs.'

'And quite right too with them murderers in the park. Old Mr Iggleby would've had 'em, if they hadn't had him. He knew how to use that pistol.'

'Did he Mary?' asked Joy. 'Did he ever have it down before?'

'Bless you yes,' said Mary. 'When he was upset. "Mary," he'd say, "I'm like the captain of a boat, and I have my weapon. We're an isolated house." '

'When did he say that?'

'When there was gypsies about. And when that foxhunt was meeting round here. And once it was some hikers. And tonight of course.'

'Tonight? What happened tonight?'

'Something upset him,' said Mary tranquilly, 'just as I say. Poor old good old gentleman.'

'Do you know what it was?'

'That he never said. But he did say, "Mary, there's villains about that nobody knows." '

' "That nobody knows"?'

'Or "knows about". Something like that. You could tell he was upset. It was eight o'clock or so, after Miss Joy was gone out and when Doctor Saintly's letter came.'

'Doctor Saintly's letter?'

'A few minutes after that maybe. The letter was sent over by hand, by that old Mr Burr, that old gardener. And he's no better than a gypsy I sometimes think. Mr Iggleby told me about it. He was upset and he had the pistol down. Small good it did him poor gentleman.'

'And you aren't sure what did upset him in the end?'

'He said "there's villains about that nobody knows". I shouldn't wonder if wasn't that Burr. Burr just went round to the library window. He never came to the door. That might upset anyone.'

'I wonder,' I said to Joy, 'about the doctor's letter?'

'Oh I can tell you that,' said Mary. 'That was about his digging and those things he finds. Beautiful, some of them are, and old. But who's to care for them now I do not know. And some of it's no more than old teeth and old rotten bits of marrow-bone. Him and the doctor, they wrote a book together. And I know he got excited about this letter tonight, because there he sat with it in front of him, reading books and looking back at it, all the evening with no supper. I went in three or four times, but he had no appetite.'

We were both stupefied by this flow of information.

'The things you know,' said Joy weakly. 'You really loved

him, Mary, didn't you?'

'Course I did. Like a child to me he was. As for the things I know, ask nothing and you'll find out nothing. Course I know things. And now I'm off to my bed, and Miss Joy you should be the same. We shall have a nasty long day tomorrow I dare say, and I shall have most of it to worry about. When can I go and clean him up and that?'

'I'm afraid the police will want to do that on their own,' said Joy. 'Ben dear, goodnight.'

'Goodnight,' I said as simply as I could.

The two ladies withdrew to their bedrooms, and I really did keep my strange vigil at the foot of the stairs. Some houses at night are deadly quiet, others breathe and stir in their sleep. Several times I heard suspicious noises, and once I tiptoed back into the library. It was no less ghastly with the passing of time. The long-case clock groaned ironically and through the broken window-pane the coldness of the mist was penetrating the house. But the night outside was perfectly silent.

I became greatly interested as I pondered and smoked away the hours in the precise contents of Doctor Saintly's letter. But that must be underneath Ralph Iggleby's dead body, I dare not tamper with it and I dared not move him. If the letter was bloodied over and indecipherable I might get Joy, or the police maybe, to ask Doctor Saintly what it said. And if there was no letter? If, when they came to search thoroughly they found no trace of any letter from Doctor Saintly in that room, then he was the murderer. As sure as death he was.

Otherwise it was a question of alibi. The vicar and Frowser were together when we met them. Ralph Iggleby would hardly think of Frowser as an old familiar friend. And Dr Stoup looked too elderly to swing that heavy weapon. And he was a Christian after all. What was it Mary said? There's villains about that nobody knows. If I could make myself invisible what would I not do? I'd be in bed with Joy at this moment, and to hell with guarding this staircase. The mist outside was beginning to lighten. It was colder. Villains about that nobody knows. I patrolled the hall to ease my stiff legs. The library summoned me again.

I had left the light on. The mule-train and the cricket teams peered sadly and ironically down. A book lay where it had fallen from the desk. It was Hendricks on *Pastoral Cultures of Early Britain*. Under it was a letter, face upwards. From Saintly, as it had to be. J.B. St. G. Saintly. Flash name for a country doctor. And a string of degrees, not all medical. And fellow of this and that. He must be a formidable scientist, whatever else he was. The letter was brief.

Dear Ralph,
After I left you last night I was looking at Hendricks, *Pastoral Cultures of Early Britain* (1962). I found on p. 363 a paragraph that you might care to look at again. The notes give very full references, but I have not had the opportunity to pursue them. I will give this letter to Mr Burr the poacher to drop in at your window this morning, or whenever, *entre le chien et le loup*, he next passes by on his wicked pursuits. Look after yourself in this bitter weather.

John Saintly

The note was dated, and Burr seemed to have taken all day to deliver it. In fact he came at dusk, as prophesied, *entre le chien et le loup*. When you couldn't tell a dog from a wolf. Twilight. What the Greeks call wolflight. The only time I ever saw a free wolf was at twilight. Villains about that nobody knows. I found myself shivering all over. This would not do, so I took Hendricks with me and the dog's blanket that still draped half of the sofa, and went back to my post.

I made little progress with Hendricks that night. One pastoral culture looks to me very like another. They make cheese in the Afghan mountains just like the cheese in the Jura. Another thing that pastoral cultures have in common is that they leave only the most modest archaeological traces. Hendricks had made a profession and a special science out of telling one from another. He was strong on the movements of flocks and the migrations of tribes, which he traced by their simple and often unimpressive pottery. He spoke not of peoples but of folk, rather an old-fashioned habit in the sixties. There were the wave-pattern cup folk and the northern beaker folk and the hooped bucket folk. The argument rightly assumes that a

43

hooped bucket or a wave-pattern cup implies an entire way of life.

The paragraph on page 363 was very suggestive indeed. I could understand why Ralph Iggleby had spent the last hours of his life searching through books. Hendricks had a spear-head or an outpost in Northamptonshire, moving north in the sixth century B.C., of some people he traced from the south coast of Britain. Later they disappeared. They died out or they settled down. The notes suggested the typical graves of these people were in the Isle of Wight. That area being notoriously open to foreign influence might explain why this people's graves, even as far inland as Northamptonshire, sometimes contained material thought to come from the Rhine. A particular kind of bone comb was what it amounted to. But the site in Northamptonshire was only twenty miles away, and the pottery sounded the same. Clever Doctor Saintly.

Or over-clever Doctor Saintly?

A ragged chorus of wet and drowsy birds. It was light. Joy came rushing downstairs with a pale face and dark rings under her eyes.

'I've run your bath,' she said. 'I'll make you coffee.'

6

Joy drove me home through the brightening daylight, and from home I telephoned the police. From the beginning I fell over my own feet with awkwardness and made the story seem stranger to them even than it was. I think I spoke to some tired, angry policeman caught at the end of night duty. I was keeping him from his bed. When the patrol car arrived at Stonehouses, things were worse.

'And when was this, sir?'

'Two in the morning I think.'

'You think, sir?'

'One or two.'

'I see, sir. And did you telephone us?'

'It was no use.'

'We had a night operator here, sir. And a night staff.'

'I mean the phone was cut off.'

'Cut off, sir? Cut off how?'

'I don't know how. Somewhere in the park I suppose.'

'That would be here, the deer park at Stonehouses?'

'That's right.'

'And yet you were speaking from here just now?'

'No, I was at home, I went home to telephone.'

'And who did you leave, sir, at the deer park?'

'A maid called Mary.'

'A maid. Alone.'

'I thought you were certain to arrive quickly. I have a great deal more to tell you.'

'All in good time, sir. If the death occurred in the night as you say, then there's no tearing hurry at this moment. The police doctor is on his way now, and other officers will be out later. Now let's have this all from the beginning if you please, sir.'

'Who is the police doctor? Can you tell me?'

'Why do you ask that, sir?'

'Is it Doctor John Saintly?'

'No sir. Doctor Skatch. Our usual police doctor. Why does that worry you sir, who it is?'

'Because Doctor Saintly might be concerned in the murder.'

'Doctor Saintly? Isn't that a very serious accusation to bring? Have you any evidence for that?'

'Of course. That is, no, not really. I mean I might have. I need to explain all this to someone in authority.'

'Yes, I think you do, sir.'

'I'm sorry officer. A man's been murdered and we're all very upset.'

'Or suicide, sir. It's not unknown. The doctor will tell us. You spoke of a gun going off.'

'Yes, I have it here. It isn't how he died.'

'You have it where, sir?'

'In the car. I took it with me for fear we might be attacked.'

'And have you a fire-arms certificate, sir, for that weapon?'

45

'No.'

'And is it loaded?'

'Yes.'

'Then I'm afraid you'll hear more of this, sir. That is a most serious offence. And why should *you* fear you might be attacked? In broad daylight on the road? Who by?'

'By the murderer. Because of something I know.'

'And what is this thing you know?'

'Something he thinks I know.'

'Know about what?'

'Don't you see? I don't understand why Ralph Iggleby was murdered and I don't know who murdered him. All I know about is his excavations.'

'And what were they, sir?'

'Archaeological excavations.'

'Ah yes, and had he maybe found something very valuable?'

That was the one useful question I remember him asking in all his endless interrogatory. But he hardly waited for an answer. He turned back to an earlier line.

'And you think Doctor Saintly has some connection with all this? You think he murdered Mr Iggleby?'

'It isn't impossible.'

'Oh no. Nothing's impossible. It might be the vicar who murdered him. Or a mad professor. Or if this was a story it might be the butler. How well did you know Mr Iggleby?'

'For a very short time. But we were friends.'

'And do you know of his having any enemies?'

'He thought he had. He took down that pistol and loaded it and he fired it.'

'Ah, the pistol again. Where did that live?'

'On the wall on two hooks.'

'And where were the bullets?'

'I have no idea. I found two on the desk.'

'And you knew how to use the weapon?'

'Yes.'

'And you still have it?'

'It's outside in the car.'

'Having been handled by you. So if that was the murder weapon, and if it carried the murderer's prints, the only prints

46

we should now expect to find would be whose?'

'Mine.'

'I was wondering when you'd see that.'

'But it isn't the weapon.'

'Is there any other? Is there one I failed to see?'

'I believe he used a cavalry sabre. There used to be two on the wall.'

'Then where is that now?'

'I don't know.'

'You are telling me that the murderer, who you think was probably Doctor Saintly, nearly cut the old man's head off with a cavalry sabre, and then ran off waving it across the park.'

'It was a misty night. And I have no idea where the sabre is.'

'We shall have to search, shan't we? We shall have to hope the day clears a little more than the night. And what were you doing walking about in this dark misty night in the park here?'

'I was with Joy. We did visit the excavation, but essentially we were just walking. The mist came up later.'

'Ah yes, the excavation.' His voice became cunning. 'And did you have a metal detector? Or any instrument of that kind?'

'Certainly not.'

'And what about the treasures you say Mr Iggleby was digging up? Are they in the bank or in this house?'

'In the library in a cupboard.'

'And nothing missing you said earlier? No theft from the library?'

'Only the sabre. Oh, and some pieces of Greek pottery. That may be relevant and I should like to make a statement about it.'

'There'll be a time for that, sir. I'm sure the inspector will want you to make a statement when the time comes. And to keep yourself available for enquiries. But meanwhile if you'll just answer my questions.'

'Of course.'

'Is this very valuable then, this Greek pottery?'

'No. Not really. It might be worth thirty or forty pounds, even a hundred.'

'Murder's been done for less, sir, and is done every day. Now if you'll just go back to the beginning.'

At last a fresh carload of policemen arrived. They bounded

out, led by an officer with a bald head and a strong, old-fashioned railwayman's face. He had large, direct grey eyes and a musing mouth. But the questioning was much the same.

He began by consulting the man from the patrol car, then with a severe stare both at him and at me he opened fire.

'If you wouldn't mind starting, sir, by telling me the whole thing in your own words, as much as you know?'

But soon it was, 'Just a moment, sir' and 'Could you explain that?' and 'Have you any evidence for that?' And then it was 'Now if you'll just go back to the beginning'. I became dazed, I began to clam up, I withdrew from every conjecture, every implication, and ended by spitting out facts like grape-pips. In fact that inspector milked me dry.

More and more policemen seemed to arrive. The wireless telephones in the police cars chattered away. Black uniformed figures spread out across the estate. The doctor arrived, and various technicians, and at last the ambulance. By that time I was between questionings, and I saw the stretcher carried out and the ambulance leave, watched by the forlorn figure of Mary with her eyes full of tears. Soon after that she was marching into the library with buckets clanking, and an over-powering smell of disinfectant filled the house. That morning I hardly spoke to Joy at all. Either she was wanted by the police or I was. We were too sad anyway, and at least in my case too dazed and exhausted, to have very much to say.

For lunch we ate sandwiches that I hardly tasted and Joy hardly touched. The police were showing less and less interest in my suspicions, and I was more and more reluctant to explain them. By the early afternoon the searchers in the park had found my bicycle, which stupidly I had forgotten to mention to them. Indeed I had forgotten its existence. What a long time ago it seemed already, that dinner and the night-ride: a time without a past and without a future. Pasternak says somewhere that 'The future is the worst of all abstractions. The future never comes in the form you expect. Or wouldn't it be truer to say that it never in fact comes at all?'

That is how I felt when they came wheeling my bicycle triumphantly back to the house, and far more so a little later, when they found the cavalry sabre still blood-stained. It had been in the brambles within easy throwing distance of the bicycle.

'And you knew, sir, you said from the beginning that the wound was made with this sabre?'

'I thought so. Because it was missing.'

'And where did you leave your bicycle?'

'And when did you leave it there?'

'Yes quite so, she does confirm it. But where exactly did you leave it?'

'And suppose I tell you it wasn't found there, but right on the far side of the park, over towards the village?'

'No, there is no mistake. That was where it was found. Yes, the sabre with it. Flung into some brambles. Without seeing the bicycle we might never have spotted the sabre. It would have rusted over, and been covered over with leaves.'

'And this other person, this murderer you heard running off. How do we know he existed?'

'Oh yes, she does confirm it. She confirms everything you say.'

'Why would she? Well now, suppose you really did leave the bicycle where you said, and then went later and took it?'

'Why? To get rid of the sabre. You or the murderer did that. Unless you are the murderer.'

'Or suppose you just agreed to leave the bicycle where you said? But you never had time to put it there? You just left it where you left the sabre?'

'When? During the early hours of this morning, when by your own account you were quite alone.'

'Then take the business of this gun. How do we know anyone fired it but you?'

'Suppose your intention was to shoot Mr Iggleby. But you missed. That's a heavy weapon. It would have a terrible kick and you aren't used to it. You might miss.'

'Where did you learn to shoot a pistol?'

'Have you ever had a fire-arms certificate?'

'How long have you and the girl known each other? How would you describe your relationship?'

'What would she have to gain from Mr Iggleby's death? Would she be his heir? Would she inherit anything?'

'Oh no. Of course it wasn't theft. That would be easy to trace, wouldn't it? Treasure like that.'

'What about this opening of a grave? Were you a party to that?'

'What about the coroner? Why was the coroner never told? What about the law on treasure trove?'

'Sleepy, are you? Yes, I should think you would be sleepy after your night's work, whichever way it goes.'

'Oh no. I'm not going to arrest you. Not now. I hope not ever. This is just an informal discussion, sir, and I'm sorry it's taken the turn it has. But you see I have to ask these questions. These coincidences are very strange. Now if you'll just go back to the beginning again. Now in your own words, how did all this start?'

At what must have been tea-time in the world outside there were two more discoveries. One was made by the police in the library. It was Ralph Iggleby's will, which was brought at once to the inspector who was examining me. The other was the fragments of the work of the Dolphin Painter. Mary found them when she went to tidy the old man's room. They were tucked into a clear plastic bag, nestling like broken eggs in a nest, inside his chamber pot. With them was a note written on a label, addressed to me. 'These are for Ben Jonson, for fear they should go astray. Keep them quiet at present.'

The will was even more of a surprise. Most of it was just what you might expect: the estate to go to a cousin, bequests of money and silver, his library to go to his old college, and so on. The only charities were the Lifeboats and Dr Barnardo's Homes. The surprise came at the end. There was a clause leaving his collection of local antiquities divided between his old friends Doctor Saintly, Doctor Stoup and Miss Beckenham. That had then been cancelled with yesterday's date, and a new clause substituted leaving his antiquities 'in view of their much greater monetary value now' to remain with the house and estate as part of the furnishings of the house. If they were ever sold the money was to go to the Society of Antiquaries of London. Joy got a hundred pounds and the car. And 'Ben Jonson of whom I have formed a high opinion' was sole literary and archaeological executor, with all rights and publication rights in his absolute discretion.

I thought somewhat wryly that I might now be in worse trouble than ever. I can think of one or two archaeologists who would murder their own grandmothers for the right to publish what Ralph Iggleby had just dug up. If it was genuine of course; and that question now rested in my sole discretion.

But luckily for me the inspector was disinclined to credit far-fetched motives. Or he had simply gone off the boil, like a kettle. The witnesses to the new part of the will were old Burr the poacher and an estate workman called Adams. That turned police attention to exact timing. Adams was found and the timing was established just as Mary had given it. They had signed as witnesses standing at the window when Burr delivered his letter. The letter was produced and meant nothing to anyone but me. At last the inspector announced his conclusion.

'That rules you out and the girl out. You were together by then in the next village, miles away in fact, when the will was altered. We shall have to find witnesses to confirm that, but I accept it. You had little to gain, and that little you knew nothing about. The girl had something to gain, but she knew nothing either. Still, I do need to be satisfied about certain points. I shall have to ask you to tell me your version of this whole story. Will you start at the beginning again and just tell me in your own way?'

I told him how tired I was. When was he going to question Dr Stoup or Dr Saintly or Miss Beckenham?

'And who is this Miss Beckenham?'

She turned out to be an elderly local lady I knew quite well. She had the best of alibis. For the last eighteen days she had been lecturing in Australia. She was an expert ethnobotanist, which means that she studied the history and the prehistory of this planet in terms of the territorial aggression of dandelions, the tribal wars of peas and beans, and the adventurous voyages of the coconut. She felt for the black rat against the grey rat, and the British elm against every substitute. She would have been a mine of information about wild gooseberries. She could not by any remote possibility have had anything to do with Ralph Iggleby's death.

Finally the police let me go. They were extending their

enquiries so they said. That must have meant the vicar and the doctor. But there was no real evidence against anyone. And one thing puzzled me badly. If there was something phoney about the grave, as I sensed that there was, the hoaxer and the murderer might not be the same person. Even in the panic-stricken moments of being found out, no hoaxer, and no mere sharp dealer like Touloupian, would use the sabre. If it was really a hoax, the hoaxer had little to lose except his reputation for gravity. But what had anyone to gain by Ralph Iggleby's death?

To me it was a heavy loss and a heavy responsibility. When the police had gone, Joy and I spent the evening together. I am afraid we simply collapsed in one another's arms and the tears trickled down our faces. Then we fell asleep.

7

When I woke the next morning it was the usual bedraggled weather. For a moment I felt happy. I was unable to remember anything. Then it all flooded back, and with it came a headache. Joy got up and made tea while I lay prostrated. Still, something was stirring in that mass of troubles, there was at least something I felt I could do. By the time Joy came back with the tea I was able to formulate it. It must seem strange to most people, but I can assure my readers that the idea of work, of an objective, laborious task which was not beyond my scope, gave me great pleasure at that moment. Whether it was my revenge on the police, or on the murderer, or on the whole distressing world, I do not know; but my intention was to study that excavation as no excavation had ever been studied before.

So I kissed Joy, and took what notes I needed, and went into Oxford. There the light grey buildings loomed under the dark grey clouds. The sooty stone walls of my college showed their usual black and yellow. Nowadays the quadrangles of colleges are more of a haven than ever before. More doors are barred against tourists, and the contrast is steep between our quiet enclosures and the debauched streets. In Cornmarket Street the crowds press uncouthly and buses prowl nose to tail. Inside the libraries, tranquillity reigns, OK? I am inclined to think the greatest privilege of working in Oxford is the possession of certain small keys. They let you through locked, secret-looking gates in high walls, out of the press of the world into stone courtyards and unlikely gardens.

It was in one of those gardens I arranged to meet Joy in the early evening. But before then I had to cover much unfamiliar ground that radiated from page 363 in *Pastoral Cultures of Early Britain*. I did cover it, in the time, and I became a convert to the belief of several quite reputable scholars that Ralph Iggleby's people must have been recent arrivals in the late sixth century. It was beyond dispute that the place to study them on the ground was the Isle of Wight. The material from their graves on that island was almost all in the British Museum. So if I wanted to test this theory fully, which sooner or later I would have to do, I must go up to London again.

There was another matter. The small golden bowl was decorated with a line of simple circles or flowers. I had never seen anything exactly like them, but that was no argument. Gold is notoriously difficult to test, because the authorities who take control of it wherever it appears are reluctant to waste a few shavings on science. Otherwise it ought in principle to be quite easy to tell where in the world any given piece of gold comes from, the alloys never being quite the same in two places. The test is really not unlike the fingerprint test for human beings, or the still more disgusting saliva test they use now. They nailed an IRA boy of seventeen with that, for a crime committed when he was fifteen. They had him in for stone-throwing and found it was his saliva that stuck the stamp on a parcel bomb, two years before. If you can do that with one lick of spit there ought to be ways of testing a golden bowl.

The gold gets brittle by being in the earth. New gold is much suppler. Microscopes will show up the structure of the metal so that you can almost watch ancient gold being infiltrated by other metals present in the soil. They soak into it, so to speak.

And of course a forger may make a mistake. I once saw a lovely island marble statuette of a woman. I saw it in a Greek village with the earth still on it, fresh out of the ground. They were trying to sell it. Only there was a break, mended with glue, underneath the mud. In the same way there's a famous golden brooch in Italy that was on display in museums for many years. It was made, we now know, by an Italian and a German working together. They used some chemical agent to treat the surface. But that brooch is supposed to have an ancient inscription on it, and the inscription was done after the agent was applied.

On the whole though, I was inclined to credit the gold. I even doubted if there was a single forgery in the entire group of things. Only that the skeleton might not be the right date. And that none of these things might really belong together. But if someone had bought the bowl only to use it for Ralph Iggleby's excavation, that was a very expensive joke, and a very expensive present to Ralph Iggleby. Then suppose they expected to get it back? By inheritance? Did anyone know what was in the will before he altered it? The best way to find out that was to ring up Miss Beckenham in Australia. What on earth time was it there?

Wandering out into the air, I ran into Frowser. He brandished his absurd moustache.

'My friend Dr Touloupian,' he said, 'asked me to speak to you.'

'Your friend? How your friend?'

'My old friend. As a matter of fact,' he said with complacency, 'we were at school together.'

'Frowser, I believe you were Touloupian's fag.'

'Nonsense. Stuff and nonsense. It wasn't that kind of school.'

'Oh?'

'No.'

'Oh.'

'I was to say how sorry he was about your head. How is it? Seems all right to me.'

'All right. He has some drawings of mine.'

'Ah. He spoke about the drawings. He said he deeply regretted to say, but in the process of cleaning up after the burglary, your drawings were unaccountably swept away. They were destroyed.'

'Who by?'

'The secretary thought they were doodles. You'll have to make them again. He's very sorry.'

'Never mind. Perhaps I shall use photographs.'

'Oh, you have some have you?'

'No, but I have the originals.'

'Really, can I see them?'

'Not your subject is it, really?'

'Not quite. But I thought there was some special secret about them. You left Dr Touloupian with that impression.'

'He left me with a sore head, which I still have.'

'What were you doing then, in the middle of the night, wandering about Ralph Iggleby's park?'

'I was with a girl.'

'As she went to the garden for parsley to stuff a rabbit.'

This allusion was lost on me at the time, which is just as well, because if I had known how rude he was being, I might have behaved really badly.

'And what were you doing there?'

'Walking with the vicar, Dr Stoup.'

'Do you know what happened at that house on that night?'

'What do you mean?'

'Have you seen today's papers?'

'No. As a matter of fact I haven't. What happened?'

Naturally, I was watching him very closely during these exchanges, and I was unable to escape the impression that he really might not know. When I told him of Ralph Iggleby's murder he went pale, he was certainly upset. When I told him in full detail what Joy and I had found he was shocked, horrified.

'And who was it? Who did this?'

'No one knows.'

'But you must know.'

'Why?'

'The police must have some idea.'

'They had none last night. When you go back to college you may find a message.'

'A message?'

'They may want to see you.'

'Oh Christ this traffic. Here, can't we get off this street?'

'Yes of course.'

'To see me because I was in the park you mean?'

'Maybe.'

'You don't suggest I'm suspected in some way?'

'I don't suggest anything.'

'But what do you think?'

'I'll tell you what I think. I think you went to dip your fingers into the water, and fell into the river. I think you know about something, or are mixed up in something, which has an obscure bearing at least on Ralph Iggleby's death. And I think now you ought to go to the police and tell them about it. And if you don't do that, if you're in any deeper, if it's worse than I think, then I shall find out, and I shall hunt you down for it.'

Frowser had gone multicoloured like a fritillary. He gasped like a carp. He inhaled and exhaled and flapped his gills. He was very angry indeed. He was on the point of speech. The smoke of his rhetoric hung heavily in the air. Without saying a word, he turned on his heel and walked away from me. I found that I was shaking too. I had probably done irreparable damage. Either Frowser was innocent or he was guilty, and in either case what I had said was excessively foolish. He was now needlessly insulted or needlessly warned. Perhaps a bit of both. He would do dreadful things. I know not what they be, but he would do them.

After that explosion, lunch in college was pleasantly soothing. It is a curious fact about Oxford that at one o'clock or half past one, thirty or forty rooms full of sober university teachers sit down in their separate conclaves to lunch; to the same colour schemes, the same kind of faces, even the same conversation, but oh what different food. While one college chews its way through stewed dinosaur and another specializes in cold rubber chicken, the fellows of the favoured colleges wrinkle their happy old noses over dark savoury messes, they dart about among the numerous cheeses like bees in the blossom. These graces of the kitchen are scattered by providence almost whimsically. A college has a magnificent cellar because one man selects it all, or excellent cooking because the old men brought up a talented kitchen boy to feed them lobster to their hearts' desire. Lunch in my college is a gentle lyrical poem on most days of the year.

The afternoon was interrupted, as so many afternoons are, but I traced most of the objects out of the tomb. I was disturbed to notice that they were exactly what could be verified from tombs of the same date elsewhere, some of them very recently published. There was nothing at all new, nothing out of place, except for the gratuitous Dolphin Painter. In the case of a genuine find, I would expect something at least to be out of the ordinary, and not everything to be so easily confirmed. There have been several cases of suspected hoaxing where the first disturbing element was a mysterious coincidence with the doctrine of the latest archaeological periodicals, and a similarity to the newest finds.

All the same, if these objects of ours were not actual forgeries, someone must have gone to great expense and trouble to bring them together. None of them was a great masterpiece of ancient art, but they were objects a museum would be happy to house and many private collectors would surely be anxious to acquire. And they would not have been on public sale in recent years, because that could be traced. Then what if they were part of an inherited collection? Or what if in fact most of them had come from one grave, or one cemetery of graves, only elsewhere? In that case what about the Isle of Wight? The pottery, like it or dislike it, seemed to match the Isle of Wight pottery.

The best place to find out quickly what is going on archaeologically in the Isle of Wight was probably the Society of Antiquaries in London. In that tall, still library they display recent copies of every local British archaeological journal, from the most massive volume to the flimsiest pamphlet. There is nowhere in my world where it takes so short a time to answer my kind of question. I wondered how often Ralph Iggleby had attended its meetings. Not so often recently perhaps. Not that they alter. At the last one I attended, there was a major-general in his nineties gathering ammunition for a salvo to be fired off against the Ordnance Survey, for their extraordinary neglect of those parts of the Roman forts of the Saxon shore which the sea covers at high tide. He had warned them about it before, he said, thirty years ago. He must have been a close contemporary of Ralph Iggleby. And I affirm my loyalty to both of them. In a way, I was Ralph Iggleby's fag.

There was little more I could do in Oxford without scientific experimentation. I was reluctant though, to hand over the bronze vessel I thought of as a milk bowl, or even the golden bowl, to the laboratory that specializes in archaeological tests. I had still not decided whether to make the story public, and the last thing I wanted was a lot of gossip about what things I had my hands on. Oxford is as rumorous as the cave of the winds. I was frightened about the press as well. They would get nothing out of Joy or Mary, and little out of the village, but a murder is a murder, and unless this one was part of a burglary then it must have some darker and more intimate motive.

And who had done the murder? What did he want? Had he finished? In what way might the Dolphin Painter give someone away? I conjectured now that the answer lay in Egypt. Someone in Egypt had the rest of the pot. He was asking too much for it and he had no particular loyalty to his client, who was probably Touloupian. What were Touloupian's special Cairo connections? Someone would know, it would take time, but in the end I would find it out. And meanwhile at least Touloupian and maybe also the murderer, if the murderer was at Stonehouses, now knew that I had the Greek pottery. Or that I said I had. I found myself actively praying to God that Frowser had not believed me.

At any moment I feared the telephone in my room might ring with more disastrous news from Stonehouses. I could hardly approach the police at this stage and ask for more protection. They could hardly provide it for long enough even if I did. What I needed was time to finish my own researches into the hoax. Then the police could have the results and things might be speeded up. I could not believe the murder and the hoax were unconnected. The murder on its own was not going to be easily solved. There was no doubt in the meanwhile that whoever had swung that ghastly sabre was extremely dangerous and swift and malevolent. I was twisting the tail of a tiger, or so it seemed to me.

Joy and I met like old lovers, in a fresh garden fenced in with hoary walls and overlooked by buildings in such a variety of styles as to resemble a child's box of architectural toys. We wandered about there in a magic circle of privacy and anonymity. Twenty years ago there were a thousand dons at Oxford, and you got to know most of them, at least by sight. Now there are more, and no one knows many. Anyway this had never been Joy's world. To her it was a dark labyrinth with enchanting resting places. To me it was an old coat I was used to wearing. We talked about that, and I confessed my folly over Frowser.

'I don't see,' she remarked judicially, 'that you did much harm. Whoever the murderer is must have known already those bits of pot were missing from the library. If he was interested in them at all.'

'If. But I don't like the idea of him still hanging about, whoever it is.'

'It may be someone miles away.'

'Who stood to gain anything?'

'Some old quarrel do you think?'

'It has to be someone who knew the house.'

'Well, what about Captain Prouter?'

'Who's he?'

'Oh, he came down today from somewhere near Liverpool. He's the cousin the estate goes to. He's arranging the funeral.'

'Oh God. What's he like?'

'The same as ever. He was always in and out. A little man with a red face and jet-black hair. A bit like a dog.'

'You don't like him?'

'It's really Mrs Prouter I don't like. She bullies Mary. Mary won't stay, I don't think. Mrs Prouter wants to fill every nook and cranny with arrangements of dried flowers. And she never stops talking. Ralph used to call her the Spouter.'

'Doesn't sound a very likely murderer.'

'Oh I don't know. Big fish lie deep. Prouter knew about those things from the grave. He went straight to them.'

'Did he now?'

'And Mary mutters about him.'

'What does she mutter?'

'Oh, only that there's things she knows.'

'Anyway it feels safer with someone like that in the house. Safer for you I mean.'

'Oh I was leaving.'

'Where are you going to stay?'

'I thought with you.'

'Joy.'

'If you'll have me of course.'

'In what sense?'

She had the grace to blush. She was a well brought up girl, was Joy. And so home we sped, but we were hardly in through the door when the phone rang thunderously.

'Prouter here. Stonehouses. What? Yes, Captain Prouter. The police gave me your number. What? Yes, the police. The inspector. Yes. Been ringing you for an hour. I say an hour. That is Mr Ben Jonson isn't it? Yes, well the police referred me to you. Do you know where Joy is? Joy? What an awful line. Normal for round here? What? Country what? Oh, country computers. Awful thought. Well everyone's disappeared, and it's most inconvenient. First Joy and now Mary. Yes the maid, Mary. Mary's gone. No, I don't know. Well, is Joy with you?'

It appeared that the Prouters had arrived by car in time for lunch. Then, soon after Joy had left for Oxford, about three in the afternoon, Mary had told them she was going over to the village with a letter. Apparently it was a letter of her own. Now it was a quarter to eight, and she was not back. She had no known relatives. Her things were still in her room. Words possibly had passed between Mary and Mrs Prouter. But no one in the village knew where Mary was, and five hours was a long time. The police were keeping their eyes open, but Captain Prouter wondered if they were taking it seriously enough. So did I.

There was nothing at all we could do about it, so Joy and I settled down together for a long, subdued evening, starting at every slight sound and watching the telephone as if it might explode.

8

Joy went back to the old house late that night. She was due to
pack up and move in with me the next day. Captain Prouter
wanted her to stay on at work until Ralph Iggleby's affairs were
finally cleared up, but there was no need to live in. She had
been as much Ralph's companion as his secretary, and now the
shadows of that house had become sour to her. The last thing
Mary was known to have done, before lunch on the day the
Prouters arrived, was to close down the blinds. The house was
like an empty sea-shell.

But the empty sea-shell had been colonized by a hermit crab.
The first thing the Spouter had done after lunch was to pull the
blinds up again. That was as soon as Joy was out of the way, and
it was then that words passed between Mary and the Spouter. I
had no ambition to enter into that quarrel, and nor had Joy, but
she felt from mere courtesy that she must spend at least the first
night in the house. There would be things Mrs Prouter might
not be able to find: household stores and the key to the garage
and so on. At the same time she had no enthusiasm for the
change of regime, and she could not enter the library without
shuddering. It still smelt of disinfectant. The window-pane was
boarded up, but not mended yet. The places where the heavy
pistol and the second sabre had hung on the wall were all too
visible.

At least Joy would be busy all day. I telephoned in the
morning rather early, and confirmed our fears. Mary had not
been found. She had gone to the village store, which was also a
sub post office, bought a second-class stamp with tight lips, and
posted a letter. After that it was as if she had dissolved, like
snow in the sunshine. She had simply vanished from the world.
She had not taken the bus and no one had seen her walking.
The police were talking about dragging the river. Suicide had
not been ruled out. No one was saying a word about Mary to
the journalists, but the police had already advised Captain

Prouter that it might be necessary to bring in the press to mount a nation-wide search. They would decide later that day or the next. Senior officers were coming down from London later in the morning. Scotland Yard, as the public call it.

I supposed, if we all travelled by train, I might pass them at Didcot going in the other direction. But I had hardly cradled the phone before it rang again. The police. Could I tell them, please, once again, about a matter I had alluded to during the questioning, but not included in my statement. The accident in the shop in London. The burglary. Yes, it was Bowen's shop, that was right. What was the significance I attributed to it? Where were these pieces of Greek pottery at the present time? Thank you, yes. They would call round for them, if convenient; they had better be in police care. And I would be asked to make a statement later. Yes, they thought tomorrow would do. If necessary I could be found at the British Museum in the afternoon. But for today the pieces of pottery ought to be locked up in a safe, or well hidden. Under a floorboard sounded fine. They rang off.

How odd about the floorboard. Somehow it didn't sound like normal police procedure. A cold sensation washed over my body. Oh my God. I rang the police.

In the end I found the inspector, and after numerous delays and checks I was told that no one from the police had telephoned me that morning. Naturally they were curious. So on my way to London I dropped in the work of the Dolphin Painter at the only police station I passed, with a brief note about Touloupian and the smashed Roman glass. In that note I pointed out how useless it would be to search his premises, because whatever he might have squirrelled away, it would be somewhere else by now.

The journey to London was a particular pleasure. It was not only that I was shot through with relief and love, and I admit anticipation, but suddenly there came a few days of pure and warm weather. I felt like a fifteenth-century prince of twenty-one, a rare feeling with me. 'Why do the shepherds shout Ut Hoy! and the lambs dance? It is an intellectual joy, the renaissance.' There were ewes in lamb in the fields, and primroses on the banks, and a heat haze over the Clumps, and once or twice enormous families of pigs. Life is like that nowadays. You have to go to London to see tall trees, you have to watch television to see the details of wild nature, you have to watch Westerns to see horses galloping that are not race-horses, and cattle moving in big herds. The alternative is to travel far and wide, which is expensive. I find the railway journey to London keeps me cheerful enough.

In some moods, not in others. In the mood I was in that day I did not even mind when my taxi was stolen by an obvious millionaire newspaper owner in dazzling black shoes, dark suit and brown hat, who said, 'City!' I got myself to Piccadilly, to the place where Fortnum and Mason sing to me like the Sirens and the traffic pounces like the Clashing Rocks. There I turned into the dull courtyard of Burlington House, where the Elgin marbles were first uncrated and shown to the public in wooden huts. People literally ran to see them opened, and among those who ran, John Constable was delayed by meeting a flock of sheep near where the Ritz now stands. The gloomy and ill-regulated car-park of Burlington House leads to the Royal Academy, but also through obscurer doorways to the Astronomers, the Geologists, the Royal Chemical Society, and the Antiquaries. I had remembered to wear a black tie for Ralph Iggleby. Black ties are not an uncommon sight in there, memorial services being, as Cyril Connolly used to say, the cocktail parties of the over-seventies.

The Isle of Wight material was far more abundant than I expected. It appears to have been a stepping-stone for many of the people who later settled in these islands, and a mounting-stone for every pirate in the unpredictable Channel. The Isle of Wight was being raided by the French as late as the sixteenth century, and in 1066 it was hardly part of England at all. It was an armed base camp for Danish commandos. From further back still in history, what the plough had turned up and the local archaeologists had hoarded had on the whole been very nice indeed. At the present time interest appeared to centre on some big groups of graves on the downs to the south of Carisbrooke Castle, in the centre of the island.

I studied the guide books and the map. I had never realized the Isle of Wight contained so many prisons, whole estates of coniferous woods masking two or three of the biggest prisons in England. And I had never noticed so many small, semi-fortified churches. I knew Cowes and the coastal towns and the dinghy-sailing water. I had seen the big ships go by heading out for New York, but as a child I had never gone beyond the Solent, or inland very far from the beach. The place for Hallstatt graves in the Isle of Wight was the downs. By no means everything had been excavated. In fact the place seemed to be an archaeological paradise, where a thorough field survey would take a year. I took some notes and some map references.

Before going on to the British Museum I telephoned again and spoke to Joy. There was still no news of Mary, and the police had very long faces. Ralph Iggleby's funeral had been arranged.

'How are you getting on with the Spouter?'

'Glad to see you this evening.'

'Busy?'

'Tiresome things. Key to the dining-room clock. Where could he have kept that?'

'Underneath it? Behind it?'

'Not behind it. I haven't looked underneath.'

'See you this evening then.'

'Shall I meet your train?'

'Where?'

'Anywhere you like. They've let me have Ralph's car. They have their own.'

'In that case why not get right away for an evening? Shall we meet at Didcot? Drive through the lanes?'

'Yes, I should love to. Hope the weather holds.'

'Hope it does.'

It was in those few casual words that we altered our lives, and stepped aside by chance from a trap whose jaws were closing. Not that the afternoon was unadventurous. I entered the British Museum keen on my research. I was beginning to have an idea about what trick was played on Ralph Iggleby, and what had gone wrong. The Isle of Wight graves were poorer, but they did contain some traces of continental influence. No one thought that was strange in the Isle of Wight. What was special at Stonehouses was the dramatic quality of what was found, and of course the suggestion, to which personally I was as open as Ralph Iggleby had been, that a pastoral or a forest people in central Britain in the sixth century B.C. might be in contact, at least indirect contact, with the Greeks.

Now suppose someone wanted to produce a group of things all from one grave, so that one item would date the others and guarantee the others. That was a common forgers' technique. Particularly when the things were made of gold. If a wonderful treasure of gold comes out of an ancient grave with some genuine pottery to date it, no one is going to question the gold. And if all that was due to happen in the Isle of Wight, suppose the mixture was a little bit too exotic for anyone to take. Suppose it was due to include some really juicy Greek treasures, and barbarian treasures as well. Why not? One big killing. Each item would raise the price of the others. What could be more useful than to point to a similar grave group in private hands, dug by a famous old man? Not published, they knew Ralph Iggleby. Not published and in no way scientifically tested, and the excavation unchecked, unphotographed, even the skeleton reburied. They were really quite safe.

Because when it was a matter of serious dispute his loyalty was where mine was. He didn't care two pence about the value of what he dug, but he cared like hell about what things were found together. So when the rabbit came out of the hat in the Isle of Wight, he would have come forward. He would have sworn that he had a rabbit of just the same kind, properly excavated and thoroughly studied. Suppose the scheme was something like that. The question remained who? Was the vicar of Stonehouses not on the point of retiring to the Isle of Wight? Touloupian would be handling the commercial side, and also supplying the genuine material. Possibly the phoney material as well. To judge from that dimly remembered phone call after I came round, he might easily be mastermind. The tone of voice was the one thing I did remember. If not the mastermind, at least the master. But not the murderer, because the murderer was a friend.

I knew little about the sections and sub-sections into which the British Museum is divided. My work there is always in the Greek and Roman department, or in what they now call the

British Library, a title which I imagine George III, who did a lot to build it up, would have relished. I decided to see John Gresham first, to get myself an introduction to whoever controlled the prehistory of the Isle of Wight. Otherwise you can spend too long in that museum straying about downstairs, looking at manuscripts of music for the zither, the knackers and the medieval fiddle. Or special exhibitions of early Polish printing in Hebrew. Or Magna Carta, nestling in some unregarded corner. I particularly like to visit the Codex Sinaiticus, which is one of the oldest manuscripts of the Bible in Greek. It was more or less stolen by a German from the monks in the Sinai desert. They were a slovenly lot, but at least they knew Greek, which is more than can be said for most of the people who have access to it now. One can get delayed a long time on the ground floor of the British Museum.

Up the stairs I bounded to find John Gresham, and it was as well I did so. He was polishing his glasses on his super-sober tie.

'Ben,' he said. 'Fancy you walking in.'

'Why do you say that?'

'That fellow you went to see, the dealer you were asking about. A shop called Bowen's.'

'And a man called Touloupian.'

'I saw him today.'

'Did he call on the department?'

'No, he was hanging about downstairs near the entrance. Waiting for someone, he said.'

'Funny you should have noticed him.'

'Oh, he came up to me. After I waved to him I mean. He asked about you.'

'What about me?'

'Were you coming to London? He wanted to see you.' He wiped his glasses.

I wondered whether to tell John Gresham the whole story. I decided at once that I was unable to face the cross-questioning that would have followed. So I just said 'how curious', and ploughed along on my course towards the early material from the Isle of Wight. I got to see it too, and it was greatly interesting. Ralph Iggleby's local pottery could have come out of one of these graves, and I began to suspect it had. Even more exciting, the circles or flowers or stars or whatever they were that ran round the rim of the golden bowl occurred as ornaments on one of two or three terracotta statuettes in the same graves. It is not rare to find the same pattern in different materials, particularly when the technique of making it is similar. It was a scratch in both cases. But the terracotta figurines were not native work. They were supposed to come from central Europe.

It was only when I left that department, with my eyes smarting as they do at the end of a day, and only when I stopped to rub them for a moment, that I had the sensation I was being followed. When I stopped, the steps stopped. I went on and stopped again, and the same happened. We were on a staircase decorated with enormous objects. No one lingers to look at them. They were too obviously chosen for size rather than beauty. Long, long ago the British Museum used to keep a stuffed giraffe in the well of the main staircase. I have always thought that a clever place to keep one. If one had a big enough house, one might keep a pair of live giraffes.

There was no doubt I was being followed. I tried several moves for a confrontation, but nothing came of any of them. The steps were firm, not even secretive. Not a woman's step. Surely Touloupian. When I asked myself why, I began to panic. It was not that I had damning evidence against him. I had none. But he obviously thought I had. Suppose I shouted to him now, 'Touloupian! Touloupian!' in that echoing place. Suppose I told him I had nothing to give him. Oh! That was it. Someone by now had tried my cottage and found nothing. There really was a loose floorboard. They would see there was nothing under it. And then?

And then Touloupian, or whoever it was, would know I had lied on the telephone. Would assume I had been lying from the beginning. Would assume I had never been taken in. Would surely assume that I knew far more than in fact I did know. The solution of my case was a grim goodnight, and swiftly turn away. I have always had a horror of falling under traffic or on to railway lines. That might easily be intended for my fate. I ran downstairs towards the King's Library, where no one is ever out of sight of the guards.

Then I felt rebuked. It may have been the people, or the light, but I believe it was the classical grandeur and the moral sobriety of the library that checked me. Why should I allow this Armenian interloper (forgive me, my Armenian readers, but that is how I then thought of him) to pursue me, to make me run? So I played hide and seek with him, round and round the postage stamp collection of King George V. I would wait motionless between two folding display boards of stamps until he moved to better his position. Then out I would rush, and he would have to bury his own head between two display boards. I must say those stamps were exquisitely uninteresting. That is one true thing about George V. It may be a dull activity to collect interesting stamps, but it must surely be virtuous to collect dull stamps. I toyed with the idea of slamming two of the folding boards together on Touloupian's head, but I thought of the guards, and the dignity of the place, and then I wondered if he might have the same idea. So I made off at a fast walk down the length of the King's Library.

Touloupian followed. It was Touloupian. He wore gloves as well, which is unusual these days. In the state of the market, as he would say. The gloves seemed sinister. I turned to face him and he moved aside. I went back to find him. There was a display of Islamic manuscripts. He was nowhere to be found. I returned towards the stamps. He was not up there. Towards the Islamic manuscripts. He was not visible. Now there was someone else watching me. Following me. No, that was my imagination. It was my own crazy behaviour that made people look at me like that.

So where was Touloupian? You will say this whole episode was imaginary, and down to that moment I might have been convinced. I was tired and strung up. If people do imagine things, then so might I imagine them, in the mood I was in. What could I do? So long as I was inside the museum, or in its vast forecourt, I was safe. Unless Touloupian had a gun hidden in an umbrella, like a Bulgarian secret agent. Why those gloves? I had read somewhere that stranglers wore gloves. Had he any accomplices? Surely. Certainly. Then he had done his part already. He had pointed me out. And now I was going to be mugged.

I became absolutely furious. I went to the postcard counter and bought a handy-sized imitation of a bronze god. I stormed out of that museum like an angry thunder-cloud; I grasped the bronze god round the neck. I believe a bottle is a better weapon, particularly a broken bottle. But I would not know how to handle one, and the police might ask why you were grasping it, and anyway you might hurt somebody with a bottle. My little god, who was otherwise unhandsome, and whom in fact I threw out of the train window outside Reading, was only meant to proclaim my fighting spirit. Who but me could know he was only made of polystyrene? For whatever reason it was, whether because Touloupian ran scared or because my plastic god frightened off his accomplices, I got safely to Paddington and on to the train. The surprise came at Didcot.

Joy was in tears. She came running along the platform and hugged me. She sobbed and sobbed.

'What is it? Joy, what is it?'

'It's Mary. And you.'

'What?'

'They've found Mary in the river. She was strangled. And her body was tied to your bicycle.'

'To my –?'

'To sink it. Some little boys found her, playing down there. Oh it's horrible, horrible.'

'Of course it is. Awful. When did it happen?'

'Wait, you haven't heard it all yet. The police want to see you. They're meeting this train at Oxford. I didn't tell them.'

I still failed to understand. 'Why not?' I asked.

'Because they think it's you. It happened yesterday afternoon when you were in Oxford. Everyone else has an alibi. Even I stopped at a garage at the roundabout. Did anyone see you in Oxford? Did they?'

'Oh my God.'

'Did no one?'

'Only Frowser before lunch. No one after. Not even the porter.'

'Well let's go. You'll simply have to hide till it's all cleared up. I'm not having you arrested. I'm just not having it.'

'They'll soon find out you were with me.'

'Not if we're clever. I know what to do. Come on.'

We hurried down the station stairs among the last of the passengers, then out into the car-park to one of the most easily identifiable motor cars I have ever seen. As we got into it Joy spoke again.

'Oh, by the way there's another thing.'

'What?'

'Your house was burgled.'

'I expected it.'

'They took up the floorboards.'

'Is that all?'

'All? Yes, it is all.'

'Joy, I think we ought to go to the police.'

'You'll regret it.'

'I think we ought to. Poor Mary.'

Joy began to cry again.

'Think about me as well,' she said.

I got her to stop the car and there in the lane we did our best to comfort each other.

9

'Can you formally identify this, sir, as your bicycle?'

'By what signs do you know it?'

'And where did you leave it?'

'When was that?'

'Was it secured?'

'How was it secured?'

'Have you any witness to that?'

The interrogation was bleak. It was seldom aggressive, but it was relentless. The worst thing about it somehow was hearing Mary referred to as 'the murdered woman'. A great deal revolved of course around what Mary knew. 'There's villains about that no one knows' was no help at all. Had she seen

Ralph Iggleby's last visitor? Or did that visitor believe so? Did she know something that only an old servant could know?

It came to me as a nasty shock that she was tied to the bicycle with four of my neck-ties. The police thought one had been used to strangle her.

'Now as to this treasure, sir, and this phone call this morning. Can you substantiate that in any way?'

'And what have you done today, sir?'

'Still this Armenian gentleman. He seems to haunt you, sir. Has he any connection with this village?'

'Only the pieces of pottery.'

'How is that exactly, sir?'

'And how do you substantiate that, sir?'

'Mr Jonson, there have been two murders done. You, on your own admission, have been connected with both. The second was done with your neck-ties, so you tell us, and the murdered woman was tied to your bicycle.'

'I don't admit the connection.'

'Don't be childish, Mr Jonson. Do you admit that you could have done this horrible crime, from the point of view of timing?'

'I don't know that. When was it done?'

'Yesterday afternoon.'

'I was in Oxford. I was interrupted a lot. Someone must remember.'

'A little after three?'

'No, I was alone then.'

'Have you any evidence of that?'

'Not really. Not that I can think of.'

'And do you accept that no one else connected with this case had the same opportunity as yourself?'

'I don't know that.'

'Miss Joy called at a garage where they know her. Not that this is a woman's crime. The doctor was treating the vicar at the vicarage. The vicar is in a state of nervous collapse, and the doctor sat with him until a nurse came. He then gave sedation. The nurse recorded that at ten to four. Too late for your theories, Mr Jonson. The murdered woman should have been back at the house by then. Your friend, Mr Frowser is it? Mr

Frowser. Your friend was in a college committee all the afternoon. Captain and Mrs Prouter were seeing the estate workman, Adams is it? And making their arrangements. I put it to you, Mr Jonson, who does it leave?'

'It leaves Mr Touloupian and half London.'

'Oh yes, there's your theory about a conspiracy. We don't like that, Mr Jonson. It's a bit fanciful isn't it? You clever men go in for that of course. Have you written books, Mr Jonson? I wouldn't be surprised. Now just go over your story again for me, from the very beginning.'

'Now what's this about Egypt, Mr Jonson? Have you been there? Quite so. And would you say Mr Iggleby had been there?'

'Then what was to prevent Mr Iggleby from picking up these Dolphin paintings himself, if that's where they came from? In his youth, if such things were known then? They were? Good. And who'd be the wiser, sir?'

This was a new possibility to me, perhaps a new insight into the whole tangle. It threw me. All I could do was congratulate the inspector.

'Ah we're not always such fools as we look, us police,' he replied comfortably. 'Even us country bumpkins. There are officers from London who may be taking over this case. But just at present I think if you answer my questions as they come, I think we can throw a lot of light on the past few days. Now to begin again.'

'Oh not Mr Touloupian, sir, not him again. This is a local crime. Whoever murdered poor Mr Iggleby knew this house. And I much doubt if it was a theft. Mrs Prouter says there's nothing missing. So did the murdered woman. So does Miss Joy. And whoever it was strangled that poor woman, the same we assume, applying great force in both cases, great force I fear, he knew her, he was a local man, familiar with this household.'

'Burr? I don't think so, sir. Have you seen Mr Burr? He has chronic rheumatism, Mr Jonson. That's a terrible thing for a gardener, believe me. They tell me he makes some of his living in other ways, and that doesn't surprise me. What does surprise me is your attitude.'

'You seem to be desperate to blame anyone, sir. You do indeed. Of course it's a frightful crime, two frightful crimes. But what will he get when we catch him? Life is what he'll get. And do you know how long life is, sir? Seven years or eight years. With two or three years' remission for quiet conduct and co-operating with the police. Now that isn't long, is it? Not for what you've done, supposing you did do it.'

'Oh but we must face that question. That's what I'm here for. We must both face it. Suppose you are guilty, you ought to consider the alternatives. There's always psychiatric evidence, Mr Jonson, and I do believe whoever murdered that poor woman is in need of psychiatric help. I'm not a vengeful man, sir, I'm a family man. And the society we live in is not vengeful, perhaps not vengeful enough.'

'Oh no, I assure you I'm not bargaining. I haven't even arrested you yet. We shall have to make examinations of you and your clothing and your house. The truth always comes out. You'll be surprised, sir, what science can do. And of course as I say it could be worse. If it were the robbery of that gold for example. Were you tempted by that, sir? I must say it almost tempts me. Wonderful thing, art. Now if a lot of money was involved I should say you might get a long sentence. Oh, up to twenty-four years. That's the way the law goes, sir. But as it is your lack of rational motive would rather tell in your favour.'

'Have you some hidden reason in all this, Mr Jonson, that I haven't understood? Were you planning to do something more? No chance of that now. None. Why don't you give up, Mr Jonson?'

I was at the lowest point I had ever sunk to in my life. My thoughts were panic-stricken. I had not even the spirit to ask for a lawyer. My only hope, and it seemed a faint one, was to stay free, to convince the police I was innocent, and to get them on my side. The Isle of Wight was a distant mirage. Joy was on the edge of being arrested as my accomplice. So far as I knew she was still somewhere in the same big police station as I was. It stood on the street that goes down to the Thames. I had known it half my life. It lay almost in the shadow of Christ Church Cathedral. But the interview room was a world as small as something on television, and Oxford Castle, where I began to foresee spending the night in prison, was less than a mile away. Boldness be my friend.

'You cannot arrest me,' I said, 'on purely circumstantial evidence.'

'Oh but we can, sir, on a holding charge. We still have that matter of the fire-arms certificate. That in itself is a crime that we take seriously, Mr Jonson. You must make your mind up to that.'

'Still, I believe in your heart of hearts you suspect I may not be guilty. If I were guilty, I think I would confess. As you said, it's surprising what science can do. There must be physical evidence that I did or did not murder Mary. May I be examined now?'

'Ah, that's a fair attitude. That's an improved attitude, if I may say so. But all that will take time. It needs a police doctor. And then there's the clothes. Just wait in here, and I'll see what can be done.'

I had appealed to science and to science I must go. They took fingerprints and nail-clippings, and they went over me as if I had been a suspected case of the black death. But they finished in the end, and I was still not arrested. I even got my clothes back. They sent me home in a police car. Joy had left Oxford long ago. She had been told not to wait, and the police found her at home when they went in to collect my yesterday's clothes. Thank God nothing had been washed.

I gave her a weak smile and a thumbs up as we passed through the kitchen. I must say something smelt good in there, and there were chopped herbs all over the place. She smiled back. One of the policemen said 'Evening, miss'. Otherwise no one spoke.

Before they left I did make one more declaration to which I had given a lot of thought.

'Can you give a message to the inspector?'

'Yes sir, we can do that.'

'By radio?'

'If it's urgent, sir.'

'Please tell him that if I am innocent, and I know that I am, the murderer has to be one of two people. He knows who they are. Tell him I want to give him a most serious and urgent warning. He must see that the doctor is never left alone again with the vicar until all this is cleared up. And to change the nurse in the vicar's house. And for God's sake to watch both of them. Because one or other of them is going to be very tempted to commit another murder, probably tonight. Tell him he may think I'm mad or guilty or both. But just to do what I said.'

'We can give him that message, sir. But I can't say what he'll do about it.'

'Never mind. Please just tell him.'

'And you'll be here, sir, when needed?'

'I shall be here.'

She had made me a vegetable pie. What an act of faith in providence, and in the British police. She had gone off to the market and found the ingredients, God knows how, because spring is not at all the easiest season for vegetables. Spring, says one of the Greek poets, when desire flares up and the knees are weak for lack of nourishment. She had burrowed about in the covered market for celery and green peppers and carrots and courgettes, and calmly driven home and waited for me. And baked this foaming great open pie, with just a little cheese on it. She had cooked it as calmly as if I was due home from the office.

'You knew I'd come then?'

'I hoped.'

'It looks wonderful.'

'I couldn't face cooking anything with blood. I hope you don't mind too much.'

'Mind? This is a feast.'

She was right about the blood, for me as well. There are those that like black puddings. The poet Auden's favourite food was long, fat, French black pudding with mashed potatoes. That is if it wasn't pork pie. The connoisseurs like all their meat *saignant*. But I would be happy if I never saw the colour of blood again. On that night I could hardly have borne it. The foulest recipe I know is a thing called Paltbread made in Denmark. They make it with rye and cloves and cinnamon compounded with a lot of blood and dark, sweet beer. They keep it all the winter over the kitchen fire-place, and they eat it soaked in hot water and smothered in white sauce. Yuk.

75

The phone rang as we were eating Joy's heavenly vegetable pie. I answered with my mouth full.

'Mr Jonson?'

'Yes.'

'I had your message. We had that alternative in mind, sir. But I thought I ought to tell you at once. Is this a bad time? No? Good, well, as I say, sir, I thought I could set your mind at rest. We have fingerprints from your bicycle. The topmost prints on it. They are definitely not yours sir. No sir, I couldn't say whose. But there's no doubt they're the murderer's. No, the river made no difference. People think fingerprints wash away, but it isn't so simple. No sir, I'm afraid they're little use. Not clear enough to trace the villain who did this. But definitely not yours. Yes, well that's all right, sir. We thought you'd like to know. The photographs have just come through. You're in the clear. But we should like to see you tomorrow, sir, if you'd hold yourself available. He may have left his prints in your house, when he took the ties. Half past eight, sir, if that's convenient.'

Joy only said, 'Of course. It was only a matter of time. Even if they'd arrested you, they'd have let you go now. We'd just have had to reheat this pie.'

As they say in the village, she had a twig in her beak. The way she reacted that evening wasn't an act of faith, it was a nesting instinct. Upstairs her things were perfectly neatly installed in the bedroom among mine. Regrettably under the circumstances, she had dusted the place as well.

'In early summer,' she said as she got into bed, 'I'll bake you a better one. With young fresh peas and beans from the garden. Fewer herbs.'

A little later she murmured dreamily, 'There's a time of year when it coincides with summer pudding. Does your bath make that gurgling noise all night?'

'You get used to it. Like the noise of trains. Or the wind in the desert.'

'No more deserts for you,' she said. 'Only bath pipes gurgling. And maybe a train or two.'

'There's a London train that you'll hear in the early morning, though the railway's miles away. It echoes up through the woods.'

76

Not that next morning. We slept the sleep of children, like John Clare asleep in a field. It was the police who woke us. They had to ring the door-bell for five minutes.

10

They were still at work in the house when the phone rang. And again, and again. It was the press. An Oxford paper. A London paper. The same London paper again. A journalist came to the door. I went down and barred the gate, which was no help really. Another fellow with a camera appeared over the garden wall. I was still not dressed, but I tried to shoo him away like shooing away a strayed hen. He gleefully photographed me in the attempt. It must have been a nice comic snap. It never appeared anywhere, luckily for me. Think how Frowser and his cronies would have relished it. Then the police took over. The journalists were shepherded outside to a kind of alarming encampment of motor cars. I took the phone off the hook.

What happened elsewhere that morning was dramatic, and although Joy and I knew nothing about it at the time, it is better to record it at this point, because otherwise what we were to go through later in the day will be unintelligible. On that morning we were happy, and worried only by the persecution of journalists. When the police left, we agreed to stay available in the afternoon and to put the telephone back on the hook. But the ringing began to drive us mad, and we decided in the late morning to break away for a few hours at least, using the same garden wall that the early journalist had climbed to capture his worm.

The dramatic episode took place in the vicarage, where the vicar had spent the night in a deep, sedated sleep. The police were watching the house, indeed they were watching the whole village of Stonehouses. But the doctor was on his rounds, as free as air. He came to the vicarage at about eleven. The policeman at the garden gate let him in, and contented himself with reporting to a patrol car up the lane. He apparently thought there was someone else inside, standing guard over the vicar. His only worry so far that morning had been a prowling journalist, and no one had told him to look out for the doctor. So in went Doctor Saintly with his black bag.

It was the nurse who realized something was wrong. Doctor Saintly examined his patient in the usual way. Then he prepared to administer what seemed to her a gigantic sedative. She asked what it was, as she ought to record it. Whatever he replied, she felt her first serious doubt then. She repeated the question, the doctor answered, and she had the sudden suspicion, even the certainty, that he was lying. The size of the hypodermic, which he produced already filled, contradicted what he said was the size of the dose.

She said, 'May I see that, doctor?'

'May you what?'

'Are you sure you aren't making a mistake?'

'What mistake?'

He could still have withdrawn.

'Isn't that a very big hypodermic for such a small dose?'

'Nonsense. It's a solution, woman. A solution.'

He looked for a vein in the old man's arm.

'But doctor . . .'

'Shut up woman.'

Then she guessed. It was something about the expression on his face, she said later. It was a contemptuous, snarling look she had never seen there before. She knew him of course. Her first thought was that the doctor had gone mad, not that the vicar was in danger. She knocked the hypodermic out of his hand, and screamed with all the capacity of her admirable country-bred lungs.

He turned on her. She thought he was about to strike her, and so probably he would have done, but a whistle was blowing and feet were pounding on the stairs. The doctor sent her sprawling with a great shove, and then he leapt like a jungle animal for the window. At the back of the vicarage an outhouse sloped away towards the garden. He was through the bedroom window in an instant and slithering down the mossy roof. He was a strong and agile man. By the time the constable had picked up the nurse and seen that the vicar was sleeping and not dead, Doctor Saintly was away through the shrubbery.

It was one of those dense thickets of laurel and berberis and mock-orange that exist in so many old rectory gardens. He knew the ground, the police in the road were not local men, and they were still beating the garden for him when he was well away into the fields. What he could hardly expect to achieve was to get back to his car or his own house. Naturally the police put up road-blocks at once. His only chance of getting clean away was going to be a long walk at night. He would have to hide the rest of the day in a dry ditch, or in the woods, and risk being found there.

Or he might have gone quite boldly into a patient's cottage; he would still have been unsuspected there. But then there was the wireless, and the risk of patrol cars down every road and lane. And it was only a matter of time before the police brought out their dogs. To avoid that danger, he would have to cross water, to take a dip in the cold, swollen river. Or to take a train. But being the man he was, he would conceive some bolder stroke. He would gamble. He would strike hard. It would be unexpected. At about that time Joy and I scrabbled over from my garden into an overgrown orchard that had snowed its blossom. We pushed through the branches of its trees for a little way until they opened on the low wall of a sunken lane. There was no one about and we dropped down into it. It was a hundred yards further on, on the churchyard path, that a bedraggled, saturnine figure stepped out from behind the vestry.

'Doctor Saintly,' said Joy.

'And this I suppose is Jonson?'

I muttered something guarded. Whichever way I flickered my eyes, I could see no journalists and no villagers. No one at all. What was he doing there? He looked as ragged as a beater on a shoot. He had been through hedges and muddy places. I asked him what he wanted.

'The fact is I've been on a long ramble across country. Getting away from all these policemen and journalists. Stonehouses is swarming with them.'

'That's what we were doing too,' said Joy.

'But I have to get home. There's a young woman who may be in labour by now. Difficult case, I ought to see about it.'

'Oh I see. Yes of course you must.'

'I wondered if Joy could run me back to Stonehouses by car? I believe you have Ralph Iggleby's car?'

'Oh well I . . . it's rather awkward.'

'Oh? Awkward? I was counting on you. I was on my way to the house now.'

Odder and odder. The way to my house was by the road. The churchyard was not a short cut, it was a long way round. Its only advantage was its secrecy. But you had to know about the sunken lane and the orchard. How did he know the lie of the land so well? And yet I had nothing positive against Doctor Saintly. If I was right about Touloupian and the Isle of Wight, Doctor Saintly was a minor accomplice. I was more suspicious of the vicar and his nervous collapse. All the same, I intended to tread carefully.

'The car's back at the house, doctor. But I'm afraid there are two or three journalists encamped there. You probably heard about my bicycle?'

'What about it?'

'Mary was found in the river, tied to it.'

'Was she indeed?'

Was it my imagination, or did I hear whistles in the distance, and the barking of dogs?

'So you want to avoid the press. Natural. Natural. But isn't there a back way in?'

Joy was firmer. 'I'm sorry Doctor Saintly,' she said icily, 'but it just isn't convenient. We were going for a walk.'

Surely, something was happening two or three fields away?

'It won't take a minute or two. Come Joy. I must get back. You can take me alone. We'll leave Jonson here if you like.'

'No doctor, that won't do.' It was my turn to be firm. If only those distant voices would come closer, whoever they were.

'I'm afraid I must insist. This is urgent.'

'And I must insist. I...'

'Young man, I have here a pistol. If you continue to make objections I shall blow this girl's head off. Move. Now. In front.

The way you came. At a steady pace. A little faster.'

He had hold of Joy by the arm, then as I started to walk he dropped back a pace or two and followed, still holding her, still holding his gun. I would not know a genuine pistol from an imitation at that distance, but it was not the moment to take any bets. As we got back into the lane, the noise of men shouting and dogs barking and the whistles diminished. They must be hunting rabbits at the edge of the woods.

The orchard that had seemed so overgrown, such a wilderness of big old trees just a few minutes ago, was a bare and open strip of ground without cover. He sat on the garden wall with his gun pointed as I crossed it first, and then Joy. When we got to the dark green Bentley, I told Joy to give him the keys.

'Not at all,' he said. 'Jonson is going to drive and Joy is going to sit behind. Get in. I shall be down here, on the floor. Is there a rug? Excellent. I shall have this gun pointed all the time. If you are stopped, you have no other passenger. If I have the slightest suspicion of you I shall not hesitate to kill. Do you understand that clearly?'

'Where shall I drive?'

'Oh, Cheltenham I think. Cheltenham and then the motorway.'

'We shall need petrol.'

'Then stop for it. But warn me in good time. For that I shall sit up, but I shall have this gun under the rug. Now, open the gates and drive out.'

We were stopped once, and asked if we had seen Doctor Saintly. The policeman knew me. No one searched the car. High up on the windy Cotswolds Saintly relaxed a little. He sat on the seat beside Joy with his pistol pointing steadily. I could see that much in the driving mirror. Apart from watching and waiting, there was nothing I could do but concentrate on the road. Soon after Burford he began to vary our route. We drove along unfrequented lanes where the car would scarcely pass. Once we drove in through the gates of a country house, and after miles and miles of avenue under trees we came out again on to a different road. No one noticed us, and I never even saw the house itself. We might be spotted somewhere, but we were not going to be easily traced. There was certainly no pursuit.

The car, to Saintly's annoyance, had no radio.

What worried me most was Joy's fate and mine whenever he should decide we had outlived our usefulness. We had done that already, I thought, when we passed the police barrier. Now it was simply a matter of his finding a convenient place. It was simply a matter of time. I prayed without hope for a puncture. The traffic increased as we came into Cheltenham, and decreased again as we made for the motorway. We stopped for petrol and drove on.

Somewhere north of Bristol we swung back towards London on the M4. We passed Bath and went on climbing into the south downs. At Newbury we turned south. As the day declined we were driving among woods on no road I had ever seen before, not far from Winchester. Joy's face was white and set. Suddenly she said we must stop.

'I think I am going to be sick.'

We were among woods. He let her lean against the wing of the car for a few moments, then she said, 'I need to do the other thing.'

For a second he hesitated. Then he pointed to a clearing in the trees.

'There, where I can see you and no one else can.'

They say that when a man points a gun at you, your opportunity comes when he approaches too close. In this case it was a question of Joy departing too far. She set off into the woods with a shaky but resolute step.

'Stop,' he said. 'There. Where you are. Stop or I fire.'

I hit him hard on the head with a hammer. Ralph Iggleby carried such things in the map pocket of the Bentley. He had a hammer, what seemed to be a chisel, and a formidable trowel. For stray excavations, I suppose, when he took a fancy for one. Arthur Evans as the *Guardian* correspondent in the Balkans once excavated two prehistoric grave-mounds before lunch, and packed off the contents to London. I found Ralph Iggleby's implements during a traffic jam in Cheltenham, and it was then I chose the hammer.

At the last moment he must have seen it out of the corner of his eye. Perhaps that saved his life. I had certainly no wish to let him live. The blow glanced off his head and hit his shoulder. He staggered and dropped the gun. He dived for it fast, but I hit him solidly with the door of the car. Then I came out hammer in hand. He lay still. I kicked away the gun from him and shouted to Joy. I was wondering whether to give him another tap with the hammer or to let him have it with a boot. Joy took the pistol and I yelled at her to stand clear.

'If you have to, shoot,' I said. Then I stood back and wondered again what to do. We were in woods and the sky was darkening. I had nothing to tie him up with, he was a desperate man, I knew now he was a murderer. He was too dangerous to take in to the police by car, even if I had the pistol. If I had reversed our positions once, then he could certainly reverse them again. Should I hit him really hard and just leave him? He was too dangerous to be left.

So I told Joy to take the car and tell the police. I could stay and guard the groggy doctor.

'And leave you alone with that man in the dark? Can you see me doing that?'

'Darling, it's worse if you're here. More dangerous.'

'Then we'll wait for another car to pass.'

It was that moment that he chose to make his move. He twisted over like a snake uncoiling. I went for him with the hammer as he knew I would. He slid around me and grabbed at it as it came. I missed him and toppled over. As I stumbled I shouted to Joy to shoot. I could feel those strangler's fingers in advance. It was all over at once. He was off with a great bound, in among the trees, as Joy was levelling the gun. There was hardly a minute to make a decision, but my half-pint of blood was up, and I went after him with my hammer.

'Get into the car,' I shouted to Joy, 'and tell the police. I'm going to keep track of him. He's too dangerous to be left.'

I could hear him crashing and thumping away ahead of me. I thought it quite likely he'd lure me into the woods and then make back for the road. He'd expect little trouble from Joy if she was alone. Or he'd stop some other car. I wondered if he knew where we were, because myself I had some idea. Winchester is archaeologically one of the best organized areas in Britain. Three or four years ago they produced a stout, book-sized pamphlet mapping and listing everything found or observed in the entire area, from a Saxon pinhead to a ruined field-system. I had spent a holiday only a year ago going over the ground with the maps and lists in hand. The noise of Saintly indicated that he knew his direction, or was he just trying to achieve distance between himself and me? Far away behind me I heard Joy driving away.

That man had the stamina of a hunted stag. When we came out of the woods I could see him far ahead, dim as the night was, flying across furrows. I was not going to be able to follow him all night. But it seemed terribly important to watch where he went. The police would want to know, and so did I. We must be somewhere near Abbotstone, somewhere near Swarraton. I plodded along more out of obstinacy than with any clear intention. Abbotstone is a deserted medieval habitation, nothing left of it but earthworks covering ten or fifteen acres. Swarraton is nothing but heavings under the turf, a lost village where only the church survived, and even that was pulled down in 1849. Places like those are thrilling on a summer's day, and best of all on a fine day in autumn, but at night alone with that murderous villain they frightened me. I gripped my hammer tightly and loped along.

I could see water. He was hidden from me now, but I had seen him turn downstream. He was going to follow the water down like a lost hill-walker. He was going to follow the river Itchen, and that would lead him into Winchester. I pulled up and stood panting. Then I listened for a long time. I could hardly hear him. Night had swallowed him up. Slowly I made my way back towards the road. The wood had been pathless; it would be worse now. I aimed to find my way round it. First I followed the line of a hedge, then the contour of a hillside. I came close to a farm where a dog barked, so I made a wide detour to avoid it. Explanations were too difficult and I had had enough of them. I thought I could see the edge of the wood, but it lay on the far side of sticky ploughland. In short I got lost.

When I did stumble on a road, I think it was the wrong one. It wound its way along like a river, it led nowhere, it was completely unfrequented. I must have wandered about until well after midnight. The lights were out in the farms and there was a hint of ground-frost. My feet were very cold. No late bus, no main road. No patrol car, no barking of police dogs, not even one old-fashioned policeman on a bicycle. Where was Joy? I hoped she was in bed by now, and I wished I was with her.

In the early hours I heard the roar of a main road and at last I came out on it. Lorries were going by, making for Southampton. That was it, Southampton. I had a surge of returning life. I would not waste time on the police in Winchester. I would go straight on to Southampton. Doctor Saintly was making for the Isle of Wight.

11

Hitch-hiking at night on lorries is not as easy as it sounds, nor perhaps as exciting. It was a long time before anyone stopped, and when he did so he gave me an extremely odd look before he let me climb in. I realized then that I was still gripping my hammer. The lorry-driver had a transistor radio, which he turned off.

'Heard about this bloke then?'

'What bloke?'

'What I said. Who they're looking for.'

'What for?'

'Murder they say it is. They say he did a strangling. And bashed some old geezer's head in with a sword. Sounds 'orrible.'

'Where did they say they were looking for him?'

'Round this way. A doctor he is, wearing dark clothes and a bit bald on top. Six foot tall and blue eyes. Not you is it? Don't sound like you.'

I must have looked terribly startled. I think my mouth dropped open.

'What's the matter then? Friend of yours is he? Seen 'im have you? In the woods?'

'No, it wasn't that. Yes I do know him though. John Saintly, is that the name?'

'That's it. That's him. A doctor like I said. From somewhere up near Oxford.'

'How much more did they say about it?'

'Well it's local radio isn't it? They don't go on a lot about it. Few jokes and another record. That's local radio for you innit?'

'But they know he's down here. Did they say anything about a car?'

'Oh yes. Yes. There was that about a car. 'E 'i-jacked a car up Oxford somewhere with a girl in it. He brought 'er down 'ere somewhere, in the Winchester area. And then 'e 'opped it.'

'Hopped it?'

'Scarpered, didn't 'e? Into them woods like I said. You see 'im in there? You're looking real worried.'

'Did they say anything about a bloke, who was with this girl?'

'No. Not on the radio they didn't. No mention of any bloke. Just this mad doctor and this girl and this old geezer and this old woman 'e strangled. Tied 'er up to a bicycle and put 'er in a river. Quite 'ard to do, that would be. I ought to know, I was in the Boy Scouts.'

A dig in the ribs and a creak of laughter.

'Well you've got to laugh, 'aven't you? Specially in this job. And things as they are. Maggy Thatcher, I bet she 'as a laugh. You've got to laugh. So 'ow did you know this bloke then? This Doctor Whatsit?'

'I hardly did know him. But I've spent half the night running after him.'

'I thought you looked a bit done in. With the police were you?'

'I was on my own. I was with the girl in that car he took. I hit him with a hammer just up the road there, but he got away.'

'Not 'ard enough. You didn't 'it 'im 'ard enough. Bastard like that, you ought to've really hit 'im. How did 'e get away?'

When I told him he sighed and shook his head. 'You're not cut out for it are you? You're not the type for it. Now if it'd been me like, I'd've put in the boot. See what I mean? You had 'im down. You should've put in the boot.'

'I suppose I'm not cut out for fighting.'

'Like I said, see. You're not the type. I see that when I first picked you up, didn't I? There you was by the roadside like an expiring fart in a thunderstorm, if you'll pardon me. I knew you wasn't no mad doctor.'

'He can't keep off the roads all night, if he wants to get anywhere.'

'Where's 'e heading for then?'

'Winchester, I think.'

'That's what they said the police reckoned. Winchester or the Channel ports, they said. They'll have 'im I'd say. They'll 'ave 'im before morning. You've no more to worry about. Where are you heading for yourself?'

'Southampton if that's all right with you.'

'Be my guest, squire. Be my guest.'

'Or if we pass a police station.'

'There'll be one in Winchester. That's that turn-off up there, where the lights are. I could take you in.'

'No there's no need really. Southampton's just as good.'

'I'd sooner not, I admit squire. Even at night getting this load through Winchester is not what I'd choose. But you only 'ave to say. Or I could get you another lift from that caff there. There's lorries pulled up there.'

'No, I'd really prefer Southampton.'

'Good then, squire. So long as we know. Like I said.'

He settled back in his seat and aimed his enormous vehicle at the coast. Southampton from Winchester is no distance at all, but before we came downhill past the ruined city walls to the shipping in Southampton Water, I was asleep. It was warm in the cab, and I knew now that my adventures were really over. I mean that was what I thought I knew.

In the end my new friend, who was a big Cockney called George, parked his truck for the rest of the night at some wire gates, and we both slept away the hours. At about eight we had tea and a bacon sandwich, then we said goodbye and I wandered away through the empty brightening streets to find a policeman.

When you are actually looking for a policeman, it takes longer than you think to find one. Then there was the bother of finding the main police station and explaining who I was. They knew all about Saintly, but nothing about me. They treated my suggestions about the Isle of Wight with tolerant sarcasm.

'Yes, sir, I see. You last saw him running towards the south, about nine or ten o'clock last night. That was some miles north of Winchester. You believe he was headed for the island ferry. And why would that be, sir?'

'Where would she be now, sir? What time of night was that when you left her, sir? She might be at home by now. It isn't much more than two and a half hours' drive, isn't Oxford, not from Winchester, with the new road. You think she'd have waited for you in Winchester? We can ask the police there, sir. She went to the police there and they'll know where she is.'

'I think we just ought to telephone to the officer in charge of the case. Will you do that, constable? Yes, Oxford, he'll still be there. Nasty crime. A very nasty experience, sir. You're well out of it. What's that? On his way is he? Yes, good, yes. It seems they're coming down here, sir, the officers in charge. They're tightening the net on that villain. The inspector asks if you'll hold yourself available for interview later in the day.'

'No sir, I don't think that's necessary. The Isle of Wight isn't Borneo you know. We have police on the island. He'd find it hard to get away from there. What he'll go for is an airport or the Channel ferry. Might try for Le Havre. Or a tour ship, there are some of them about. Or he might go to ground. Wait until it blows over. If he does that we shall have him, never you fear. But I don't see any reason to set a particular watch on the island ferry. Not from anything you've told me, sir.'

'Yes of course you can, sir. The Dolphin, you'll find, is a good hotel. Sound, not flashy. A bit on the sleepy side. Rather what you want after a night in a lorry. But if you wouldn't mind reporting back here in let's say two hours' time?'

Thank God for a credit card. The one I use is among the least glamorous and the least potent, but without it I would have been badly stuck. I fitted myself out and cleaned myself up and made a number of phone calls. I traced Joy to a hotel in Winchester near the Cathedral, but by the time I telephoned she had already left. I found out from home that Dr Stoup had come round at last, and been seen in the village pottering about. Captain Prouter named a day for Ralph Iggleby's funeral and Mary's. There would have to be a formal inquest, but the funeral was in six days' time, after the weekend. In case Dr Stoup might not be well enough, they had already found a substitute minister. Most of the journalists had gone. The nurse and the vicar refused to speak to them. 'Quite right too,' said Captain Prouter.

The air of Southampton is bright and buoyant. The sun, when it appears at all, strikes hotter on the skin than it does inland, and the town, at least the part of it nearest the docks, is full of brilliant light. Throughout the days of all these adventures, I felt continual surges of optimism. Because of my illusions? I believe that like the police, I am not such a fool as I look. But yes, all the same, because of my illusions. Because it was spring for a few moments, and even the weather was better than it had been. And because I was in love. My feelings about Joy were now a rich and dense mixture. I no longer wished to disentangle them. I just wanted her company for ever. And especially now, in the fine air.

The police officer took me gently, firmly and thoroughly over every detail of what had happened. That is probably why I remember it so well today. He took me back by car to where the lorry-driver had picked me up. He retraced every road I had taken until we came to the fields of last night. We pored over maps, and drove around lanes, and asked questions at farms, until he knew just where I had been. He identified the farm where the dog barked, the river and the wood. He pinpointed the exact spot where I left Joy. It all took an incredibly short time. The combination of Ordnance Survey maps and a local police driver reduced last night's insuperable problems and endless distances to childish obstacles and short drives. We were back in Southampton well before lunch-time.

He was not the officer in charge of the case. They had set up a headquarters at Winchester where the decisions were made and information was co-ordinated. This was not so big a murder case, nor had it lasted so long, as to call into existence the whole paraphernalia of modern police enquiry, with its huge digestive mechanism, its slow inevitable progress, and its possibilities of human error. This was a small operation directed in a smooth and deadly style by experts. It was essentially a winning game of draughts. I am not a good chess or draughts or backgammon player, because I am always distracted and I lack the killer instinct. As some professional golfer put it the other day in a magazine, how can you keep your killer instinct if you are hungry for love? But the police were not distracted. They knew just what they were doing.

I say this in their defence, because they ought to have taken me more seriously over the Isle of Wight. On the other hand, as my officer pointed out, the Isle of Wight was only a particular corner of the area they were already watching. Their man – he referred to Saintly not as 'that villain' but as 'chummy' or 'our chum' – might surface in Liverpool or in Llandudno. The first task was to deny his freedom of movement out of Britain, and the next was to confine him to a small area.

'You can think of prison, sir, as just a rather smaller area than Southampton, and a little less dangerous to the public.'

'And the Isle of Wight?'

'I have two points to put to you about that. The first is that whatever his scheme was, if it extended beyond Stonehouses, he can hardly continue with it now. To that extent he does already lack liberty. As for this other excavation, this new false treasure, we have only your conjecture that it is false. You admit the Stonehouses treasure is quite genuine. Whether it was found in the right place would interest only a scientist. We usually find that financial considerations are more important. Your scheme is terribly elaborate. I think we shall find the motive was greed. It usually is. Our chum thought he was going to inherit some valuable property. He never knew the will was changed. Or if he did find out, say from Mr Burr the gardener, then he killed Mr Iggleby out of fury.'

'I can't gainsay that. You may be right.'

'Well sir, time will tell. We shall soon know. Then I have my second point to put to you. Supposing all you say about this scheme depending on the second excavation is true. I don't say it isn't ingenious. And these are ingenious people. I admit that. And I admit that as you say it's happened before. I know my way around criminal records, and this is something I never happen to have come across, but it's your trade sir, your specialization, and I respect a man's specialization. I agree with the examples you give, and I'm grateful to have them. But does it have to be the Isle of Wight? Were these Hallstatt people not all over England? Why not in those river valleys north of Winchester?'

'Why not indeed? It was just the pottery that happens to be recorded. If you were going to produce a treasure you'd want nothing suspicious about it. You'd want it to come from somewhere well known. Where the pottery had already been studied and you only had to produce another example of it.'

'And then, what connection has our chum with the Isle of Wight? No known connection.'

'No, it's the vicar who has that.'

'And he tried to murder the vicar. That's the crime we shall hold him for.'

'He what?'

'Ah, you don't know. But that's why he ran. That's why he took your car. He'd been caught in the act.'

I was stupefied. When the officer had told me the story of the doctor and the vicar I felt that my Isle of Wight theory was terribly threadbare. I did suggest it might have been a quarrel between thieves, and my policeman agreed it might be so. It did look as if the vicar had agreed to be Saintly's alibi for the time of Mary's murder. On the other hand, there were several witnesses to the vicar's nervous collapse, and Saintly's motive for putting the vicar to sleep with a needle must surely be that he thought the vicar unreliable. We might never know the truth. At best it would be one man's word against another's.

It was the London policeman's own suggestion that I should go over to the Isle of Wight and satisfy myself. 'Just about the archaeology,' he said. 'See what's stirring. Go and have a look at this place on the downs. And keep in touch with us. Now here's my number.'

Maybe he only wanted me out of the way. But I took the Isle of Wight hovercraft in the early afternoon, passed by the glittering yachts, and landed among the unromantic mudbanks of East Cowes. I phoned from there, leaving messages for Joy at every address I could think of, and booked a room inland at a smart old hotel George V had used in Newport at the head of the Medina river. Cowes is a little cluster of old houses on both sides of the Medina estuary. It faces north across the Solent towards the vast expanse of Southampton Water. The Medina is not really so much a river as a long inlet of the sea between low hills. At the head of the Medina river lies Newport, hardly a port at all nowadays, and above and behind Newport stands Carisbrooke Castle.

It was high tide, and I stood for a few moments at the water's edge to see the yachts bobbing and dipping in the estuary. A motor launch was coming upriver from the Solent, not a big, sea-going craft but the sort of boat people buy for messing about in at the weekend. It was coming quite fast for those crowded, busy waters, like a Venice water taxi. Cowes is a kind of British Venice, I suppose. The same brightness, the elderly paint, the marine light. Well, it was the nearest we could come to Venice in the nineteenth century. The truest British Venice is the Portmeirion Hotel I have no doubt.

That boat was coming right up the river, past all the moorings, and the landing-stages, towards Newport. My eyes widened. He was wearing an oilskin and dark glasses and a cap. But surely, he was Saintly? How on earth had he done it? Taken a boat from one of these little private docks on the Hamble estuary, somewhere like that? Or his own boat. For all I knew it was his own boat. Plenty of people live inland and keep a little boat down here. He swept away out of sight at the same speed, illegally fast. I was more or less certain I had not been noticed. Thank God for the new outfit, bought in Southampton. I rushed for a telephone and found one beside the car-park where traffic queued for the ferry.

I had to wait some time because the phone box was occupied. Finally I lost patience and ran across to an office where I demanded to telephone the police. Of course the girl behind the desk was thrilled. She asked if my car had been stolen. When she heard what I did have to say to the police her eyes became starry. She went and got me Nescafé, which I loathe. When I confessed to the police that I could not describe the boat except that it was brown, a light brown colour like a Venetian water taxi, she never blanched. Was there anything else she could do for me? Would I like a chair to sit down on and wait for the police? Was I sure it was really him? She shuddered deliciously.

'It was him all right,' I told her. 'Oh, and thank you. And for the coffee.'

'It's a pleasure Eh'm sure.'

I shut the door and stepped out again into the world. The same cars were still queueing as patiently. The same boats were still bobbing and dipping in the tide. The sun still glittered. It seemed there was nothing I could better do than go to Newport and check in at the hotel. They had said something about bookings by telephone not being held after six in the evening. They spoke of 'the island'. 'Are you already in the island, sir? Oh then that will be all right.' It gave one a smug feeling. Otherwise I might have stayed in Cowes, watching the ferries and the hovercraft and the seagulls until Joy arrived.

I had the idea of taking a bus halfway up the east side of the Medina river, and then perhaps walking to Newport across the fields. I was not likely to encounter Saintly again, even if that really had been him. The boat had been headed for somewhere precise. He had a house or a friend or a hideout somewhere up there. It would not take the local police long to find him now, maybe not even the length'of a spring afternoon. Before I took the bus inland, I had the satisfaction of seeing a police launch going upriver at a slow, steady pace.

What happened after that was just a coincidence of names. I had not even started walking. The bus had gone by the gates of Osborne House, where Queen Victoria, that wicked old woman, locked herself away for years, contriving to interview Gladstone only after the Navy had made him seasick on the Solent. He fell for it every time. I was staring out of the bus windows at nothing much, there being no great open view such as I was hoping for. We dawdled uphill past the painted board that advertised a girls' private school. Recognized by the Ministry of Education. Headmistress Miss A. Stoup. Matron Miss R. Saintly.

12

Coincidences of names do constantly happen. There are fishmongers called Mr Salmon and Tax Inspectors called Mr Grab and so on. In today's newspaper, which I have just read, there was a Persian Member of Parliament called Mr Tatabaibai. He was blown up by extremists. In the case of the names on the Isle of Wight, one coincidence explains another. The mysterious Isle of Wight connection was not merely archaeological, it was a family link. Who had introduced the Rev Dr Stoup to Ralph Iggleby in the first place? It was going to turn out to be Doctor John Saintly. I left my seat hastily and rang the bell, and got off the bus at the next stop. It was at the top of the hill, in rather undisturbed country.

As I think back on that day I wonder why I failed to ring the police again at once. The true reason why is that I was sure these two ladies would not consciously be hiding a murderer. Certainly not in a school full of little girls. They would have heard the news on the wireless or else someone would have told them. Bad news spreads quicker than good. Someone would have said, 'Isn't that your brother? And Miss Stoup's cousin? Didn't we meet him? Just fancy. Perhaps he's innocent. They just said the police were looking for him. Anxious to interview him. Yes, they gave a description. I'm sure it is the same.'

Anyway there was no telephone around, the bus would take a long time to reach Newport, and time was important. What I had to do was to warn the two ladies that Saintly was heading this way. After that, it was a matter between them and the police. But suppose Saintly was going to take hostages? Suppose he had already arrived? I could do no more than hurry. The nearest telephone would be inside the school.

It was an early-Victorian building in classic taste, a little tired of life, the trees around it a little mothy, the garden carefully planted with aubretia and spiky little tulips; it was without charm. Beside the school on the hillside there lay tennis courts of that hideous pink that goes with tennis courts, and a games field much like a paddock only smaller. Beyond that and behind the house two or three ponies were grazing away in unkempt meadows that sloped down towards the Medina river. The road and the river ran close together. It was only the hedge that made one invisible from the other.

I took the obvious first step of walking around the outside of the school until I had a clear view of the water. There was no motor boat like a Venetian taxi that I could see. Neither moored nor out in midwater. And there was no boathouse at the bottom of the fields. I remember that the tide was falling. The school seemed quite deserted until I went back to the front and rang the bell. It was answered by a schoolgirl of about fifteen with her head on one side and a voice that suggested elocution lessons.

'Good afternoon,' she said. '*Good* afternoon. Do come in. Are you the new parent? I'm afraid I've forgotten your name.'

'Not really.'

'Oh that's a pity. If you were, we could have had tea. I've made it.'

'I really wanted to see the headmistress. Or the matron.'

'Oh, they're out,' she said. 'Everyone's out but me and Sabrina.'

'Oh dear, perhaps I could wait for them.'

'We could have tea anyway. And I could show you round. If you like. Since I made it anyway, because it is tea-time and I don't expect this new parent is ever coming, if you're not him.'

'Where is everyone?'

'Oh, Miss Stoup has taken everyone swimming in Southampton. We do that a lot.'

'Do you?'

'Mm.' Giggle. 'She says it develops the bosoms.'

'And does the matron go as well?'

'It's her day off. We call Friday Miss Saintly's sex life. She must have one, mustn't she? So it must be on Fridays.'

'Not necessarily.' I put this in with what I hoped was a severe tone. 'Not necessarily at all. There are plenty of unmarried people.'

'Oh nuns and so on, of course there are. Miss Stoup for

instance. Miss Stoup is very holy. She's a vicar's sister. But Miss Saintly's different. Do you know her?'

'Not really, no.'

'Why don't I show you around? And then have tea?'

The alarming child conducted me over the house with a series of prepared speeches. 'These are the original banisters which we stripped down. We do a lot of that kind of work, and most of the polishing and light cleaning. We cook too.'

'This is the rabbit warren. Well, we call it that. It used to be maids' rooms, but Miss Stoup subdivided it and put in bunks. Two girls to a room. I share with Sabrina, but she's in the sick bay today, with a cold. We get a lot of them.'

'Do I get shown the sick bay?'

'Oh no, that's Miss Saintly's pad, we call it. We're not allowed in there, for fear of catching each other's colds.'

'And what about poor Miss Saintly?'

'She drinks gin. Like my parents. *They* never get colds. Shall we have tea?'

'When will the others be back?'

'Not till six.'

'I have to book into my hotel before that.'

'We don't have to wait for them anyway. This is a special tea, because you're a visitor.'

So we sat in a pretty little room and she poured out tea like a lady. We were just settling down to it when the door-bell rang.

'Help!' she said. 'The new parent! Never mind, we'll just give him tea and show him round later.'

But it was two plain-clothes policemen, asking for Miss Saintly and Miss Stoup. I could hear every word said.

'Whatever have they done?'

'Nothing, miss. Nothing like that at all.'

'Who's in authority here, miss, if they're out?'

'I am.'

'Are you alone?'

'No, there's my friend Sabrina. She's in bed with a cold. And I'm expecting a new parent. I thought you were him actually. And I have another visitor.'

'Who's that, miss?'

'I don't know really. He didn't tell me. He's not a parent.'

'What kind of man is he, miss, to look at?'

'Tall. Quite old. New sort of clothes.'

'I see, miss, and where did he come from?'

'Well, that was the odd thing really. I was looking out of the front window because I'd made the tea, all but the tea itself, and I was expecting this new parent. This man didn't seem to come from the drive but across the fields or something.'

'And where is he now, miss?'

'Having tea. Would you like some?'

For two panic-stricken seconds I wanted to dive through the window and run away. They passed, as such moments do, and the two detectives came into the room.

'And may I ask, sir, what your business was at the school?'

I asked them to take me out to the car. The little girl watched us go, goggle-eyed with curiosity.

'Oh, that was you was it?'

'And you just spotted it, from the bus?'

'Well, as you see, sir, we'd have got round to it nearly as soon, but there's no harm done. Of course as soon as they said Winchester we began to wonder. Because the local force recognized the names, naturally.'

'No sir, the vicar's name wasn't published to the public, not by us anyway. But of course the police in every place get full details of a case like this.'

'No, I don't believe we shall see him around here sir. Not round this school. But those two ladies may have an idea where we ought to look for him. A little holiday cottage I shouldn't wonder, sir, on the south of the island. Somewhere quiet. No one about at this season. Nothing open.'

'Yes sir, that's it. He won't get off the island. Not now. With the prisons we have here, it wouldn't be the first time we've hunted a man down on the Isle of Wight.'

'Can we drop you anywhere, sir? We can call back here later.'

So I arrived in style at the hotel in Newport, and Joy arrived there soon afterwards, having picked up my message in Winchester. People even commute to London from the Isle of Wight, and commuting to the mainland is extremely common. They even have a rush-hour on Southampton Water. Seeing Joy again was like seeing her for the first time, and yet it was like the end of a long journey.

> Was never pike wallowed in galantine
> As I in love am wallowed and enwound.

Joy and I passed a long, slow evening walking about in the prettier streets of Newport, which are eighteenth-century with the charm of novelty and southern, marine light. We ate unremarkably and drank the kind of good unpretentious wine one is lucky to find now. Late in the evening I telephoned the police to tell them about our plans for tomorrow, to check that they knew where we both were, and to ask for news. There was no new development. Saintly's sister and Stoup's sister had been told, and the police were keeping an eye on the school. But the motor boat had not been identified, and no one but me had seen the murderous doctor on the Isle of Wight. The only confirmation that I really did see him was the theft of a motor boat which sounded like the same one from a private dock on the river Hamble. We might have better luck tomorrow.

And sure enough, the boat was identified early next day. Joy and I were still at breakfast when a police car came to the door of the hotel.

'We knew you were going out later, sir. Good of you to tell us. We have the boat that was missing. If you could come and confirm whether it's the same one, that would be a great help to us. Put us on solid ground.'

Joy and I went together, by river most of the way. Reaching any given point on the Medina by land can entail a longish walk, and the ground was muddy that spring.

It was the same boat all right. She still had the air of a water taxi, but a taxi smashed up. She lay half in, half out of the water with her nose stuck among catmint and reeds on a mudbank overshaded by small trees. The police theory was that she crashed empty. Saintly had contrived to open the throttle and let her go, and she must have travelled some distance at some speed before she hit the bank.

The Medina river is comparatively straight, it curves only slowly. Still, it was remarkable how close the wreck lay to the school. The school stood out white on its hillside on the far side of the river. It looked distant but it was only a mile or so away. One of the police remarked that that school might be worth a closer look.

That was no problem of mine, or it seemed not to be. I think that the rest of my adventure would have turned out just the same whatever happened at the school. But here again it is best to record things as far as possible in the order in which they happened.

Saintly had been in the school and his stolen boat was already smashed in the reeds when I first rang the door-bell. He knew the school of course, and he entered it without bothering to disguise himself. He went straight to his sister's department as a doctor, and the child who opened the door to me simply forgot that the doctor had been and visited her friend Sabrina. One or another doctor called every day. It was a piece of luck for Saintly that the sick-bay was not empty, but school sick-bays seldom are. Having once got in, he stayed.

When his sister got home late that night and saw him, she must have needed her slug of gin. One of the unsatisfactory elements in this case, when one tries to reconstruct it imaginatively from the beginning, is that the relation between Saintly and his sister remains obscure. They had certainly once been close. She would certainly have liked a more luxurious life. But few sisters will betray their only brother to the police, whatever his crime. And few women, locked up alone with him for the night, would have been unafraid of Saintly during those hours.

In the morning she must have suffered both from her feelings and from the suppression of them, when Miss Stoup calmly called the whole school together and asked the prayers of the assembly for her own brother and for Miss Saintly's. In a muted sort of way she told them the whole story as far as the police knew it. She asked them all to keep their eyes skinned and report every stranger to her personally at once. She did all that without causing a panic or even a great sensation. They took it seriously like good little Christians. She had that genius for being undramatic that ladies of her stamp and her generation sometimes do have. I believe she was a remarkable woman.

Still nothing gave. So far as I can see, that wicked villain could have stayed up there in his sister's rooms for a long time, and it might all have ended very badly. But every day of every term Miss Stoup visited the sick. So on this day she asked Miss Saintly who was up there, and Miss Saintly panicked and said no one was up there. So Miss Stoup asked was Sabrina better.

'Oh yes. Since yesterday.'

'Really? But she wasn't at assembly.'

'I know she's somewhere about.'

'But this is most serious.' And she rang one of those little brass bells they have.

'Catriona, have you seen Sabrina today?'

'No ma'am. Isn't she in the infirmary?'

'Apparently not.'

'Well, her bed in her room hasn't been slept in, because I looked.' Saturday was clean sheets.

'Catriona, fetch me her friend. Fetch me the girl she shares with, Georgina.'

'Yes, ma'am.'

And so not wanting to be caught out, Miss Saintly clasped her hands to her head and said, 'But *what* a fool I am! I only *meant* to send her down, but I forgot. But I've had *so* much worry.' And then she wept. Howled like a little girl. So Miss Stoup comforted her of course, and sent Georgina back to class at once, and gave Miss Saintly a powerful tot of gin. She knew her own matron.

Then she left Roberta Saintly sobbing into the gin glass at eleven in the morning, and marched off to see Sabrina on her own. When the brother heard someone opening the sick-bay door he thought it was his sister and called out to her. So then Miss Stoup knew. And what was her reaction? She ignored him utterly, and that may have saved her life. She yelled out in a voice of doom, 'Sabrina! Put on your dressing-gown child, and your slippers, and come down with me at once.'

'Yes ma'am.'

Then she had someone call in the constable from the games field or paddock or whatever it was, and in ten minutes' time after that the police broke into the room where the doctor sat. But he saw them out of the window first, or he heard them outside the door. They never said 'We're coming in,' but if they had done it would have made no difference, by then. He killed himself with a pill of some kind. He died extremely fast. It was all over by the time we were passing by in the launch, just when one of our policemen was saying the school was worth a closer look.

We heard the whole story later in the day, because Joy insisted that we went and called on Miss Stoup and Miss Saintly, to commiserate. She had been a neighbour of their brothers after all, and she thought they might value the gesture. She wanted just to leave a note, but we were shown in willy-nilly. Miss Stoup and Miss Saintly told the story antiphonally, like two sides of a choir, gin side and sober side. I seldom saw two such remarkable ladies. And yet I am still not sure of Miss Saintly's innocence. What I am sure of is that Miss Stoup knew much more than she said.

She did happen to let out one interesting crumb of information. The boys' school where her brother used to be chaplain was another Isle of Wight school, not far away. She said she was expecting her brother any time now, for a rest.

He needed it, poor man. Perhaps he should have retired long ago, long ago. But now he was building a retirement cottage south of Carisbrooke on the road through the downs. A tranquil spot near the best prehistoric mounds in the island. Had I any interest in archaeology?

13

Sunday morning opened like a flower in 1913, in complete calmness. Almost no tourists penetrated the heart of the island at that season. In the town, almost no traffic circulated. Ralph Iggleby's Bentley had the lanes to itself. We drove away past the tough little stub of a fortified church tower. Inside the church the service was buzzing and chanting. We thought of going in, but at that moment the parson began to preach. Not unto us O Lord, not unto us. We took a footpath up on to the downs.

With the modern mania for concentrating all hikers and walkers into one route, a sort of scenic pedestrian motorway, the authorities of the Isle of Wight have marked out something they call the Tennyson Way, which straggles for miles over the western and central parts of the island. So long as you avoid that, if you have a taste for solitude, the interior of the Isle of Wight is still unfrequented and offers continual pleasures. The woods we climbed through were dense and sheltering. They smelt deliciously of spring, and they had that slightly tropical air which clings like a green fur to the southernmost extremities of Britain.

Joy thought the police might very likely close the case with Saintly's suicide.

'It was convenient for them in a way,' she observed.

'There are questions we can never ask him now.'

'I know. Suppose he wasn't guilty?'

'How not guilty?'

'Suppose someone else killed Ralph.'

'Who?'

'Well, I don't know who. The vicar? Frowser?'

'And Mary? That couldn't be Frowser because he spent all afternoon at a meeting.'

'Nasty piece of work though.'

'So is Touloupian.'

'Funny them both being at school here.'

'Nothing follows from it.' I was unwilling to follow any more convolutions.

'Except that they know the island.'

'Except that.'

'It's odd that everyone we ever suspected should know the Isle of Wight.'

'We know it too. Half southern England knows it I expect. My hair-cutter at Trumper's used to come from Hayling Island. He used to commute between Hayling Island and London every day.'

'I'm not satisfied. Are you?' Joy said it with some finality.

'No.' I had to admit it. 'No, I'm not. And it isn't only the archaeology. It's Touloupian. And whether the vicar might be as guilty as the doctor.'

'I think the vicar knew about Ralph Iggleby's death,' she went on.

'I think he either saw it or knew who did it. And if there was any funny business about the archaeology, I'm sure he knew about that from the beginning. But Mary was too much for him. The doctor did that murder and the vicar was horrified.'

'I wonder how the timing works?'

'What if Mary went to see the vicar? Who was her letter to, that she sent? It must have got somewhere by now, even if it did have a second-class stamp.'

'How odd to think it was only last Wednesday.'

'We've only known each other about a week.'

'It feels a long, long time.'

'I feel like an old married couple.'

'So do I,' I said, and we walked along for a time in silence. All the same, the shadow of the murders had cast a chill over the day. We had been careful earlier to avoid the Sunday papers. But of course it was not possible to forget, even for five minutes. I already had some foreboding that the whole story would end as unpleasantly as it began. The pricking of my thumbs warned me of a danger that my conscious mind suppressed. We were in something like the position of those Freud says are condemned to repeat their mistakes because they have never understood them.

I felt better on top of the downs. It was a mild, sparkling morning, and we saw new lambs with their mothers in the lower fields. The mounds of the ancient people, most of them robbed or excavated long ago, looked as old as the hills were. I have read that the beautiful flowing lines of the downs in southern England took their shape from the action of water. They were once the floor of a shallow sea, a sort of underwater sand-dunes of marine deposits. The reason why some of the downs look like the hulls of upturned boats is that the boats, like the hills, owe their shape to the force and flow of water. I like to believe that sort of thing. It represents the only kind of understanding I can manage.

We came to no conclusion on the hill-top about the mystery that was engulfing us. It did us some good though to talk about it together, and we went back to the car in a more practical frame of mind. I was going to continue my researches. I knew exactly what I was going to look for. And Joy was going to pursue a suspicion of her own. After a normal hotel Sunday lunch, which cannot be helped so one might as well enjoy it, we looked at the little museum in Carisbrooke Castle which the British Museum had told me about. Carisbrooke is a romantic ruin with plenty of walls and just enough rooms left intact to give an impression of survival. It contains a children's zoo, a musical instrument belonging to one of the children of Charles I, and Tennyson's scarred and inky library writing table, rather like Ralph Iggleby's only smaller. It also has some of the surprisingly fine material from the prehistoric grave-mounds.

From Carisbrooke on its hill-top, which is really the northernmost point of the downs, we went on to explore the old mounds. Everything was undisturbed and as it had been for centuries. I checked off site after site against the map, and they were all as they should be. The one excitement came in the late afternoon at a lower level, not far from the road. There appeared to be a mound the map had not recorded. Someone had been clearing the ground of trees and undergrowth. It looked as if the swelling of the ground had been overgrown for years and unnoticed. I climbed down for a closer look.

'Here! You can't go in there! That's private land!'

In my stupid enthusiasm I had overlooked a small, furious fellow in blazing brown and white tweeds. He had a dog.

'Here! Where did you come from anyway? You can't go up there either.'

'I'm sorry. I've left my wife up there. I shall have to go back.'

'The sheep are lambing.'

'Not up there.'

'All over the downs. Damn tourists! Why can't you keep to Tennyson's Way?'

'I've been looking at the mounds. There is a path up there according to the map.'

'Mounds? What mounds? Who are you anyway?'

Something snapped inside me.

'Jonson. And who are you anyway?'

'Who am I? Biggleswade, that's who I am. Down Caesar. Down boy. I'm the agent for this land.'

'All of it?'

'Just this bit actually.'

'Who owns it?'

'It isn't for sale. It's building land, and it's been bought.'

'May I go and look at that mound?'

'Mound? That's not a damn mound. Yes I suppose you can, since you ask. Just a bit of rising ground. Soon have that level. Trouble enough here with planning permission, without prehistoric mounds.'

'Really? It doesn't look natural to me though. Does it to you?'

'Course it does.'

'It's certainly been here some time.'

'Course it has.'

His eyes were like tinned gooseberries, his face unwholesome, his brows furious. The dog Caesar was growling and pulling at his chain.

'Could you tell me whose house this is going to be?'

'The Reverend Stoup. A retired vicar from the Midlands.'

'I should think it would suit him. A quiet valley, and sheltered, and a nice view.'

'Suit him? Of course it will suit him. He bought it, didn't he? And always messing about here, every summer. Cleared the ground himself you know. Wouldn't let me bring in men. "No," he said, "I'll do it. I'll think of my congregation and I'll hack it all clear." Stuck in my mind, that.'

'I should think it would.'

'Mind you, he swings a good axe, that vicar does. Full-sized felling axe. Can't think where he got it. And treated that mound thing as if it was made of glass. Said the same as you about it, as a matter of fact. "Vicar," I said to him, "keep quiet about it, or we'll have more trouble with the planning people. The way things are." '

'Yes you might at that. What's he going to do then, leave it?'

'Oh I expect I'll level it for him in the end. Bring in a bulldozer. He said he'd dig it away this summer, but what's he going to do with the earth? "And the way building costs are going up," I said to him, "You ought to get your house built now." What with taxes and VAT and cost of materials, you know how it is. And those planning people, they're devils.'

'Yes, well. I see my wife waving to me. I'd better climb back up there. Sorry I trespassed.'

'Sorry I bawled at you old boy. Here, Caesar, back, down damn you. To heel.'

On the way home to the hotel I told Joy the news.

'But are you sure that's a genuine grave-mound?'

'As sure as I can be without looking inside.'

'And has it been disturbed?'

'Terribly hard to tell. The surface is broken where he's pulled up the undergrowth and rooted out a tree.'

'So they might have fiddled it already.'

'Quite neatly if so.'

'But will they have put the things in the right place?'

'I don't think that matters.'

'Won't it have to fool the experts?'

'No, not really. It won't be an excavation. It will be this old retired vicar clearing away a mound from the end of his garden. When it turns out to be a grave-mound no one will be more surprised than him. Quite likely bulldozers will be due a few days after that, to level the site. There won't be any evidence for any experts, only what he takes out of the mound before he flattens it. He won't report it until too late.'

'I wonder if he knew when he bought the land.'

'All this must have been simmering in someone's head for years. But whose?'

'And did they always mean to kill poor Ralph Iggleby?'

'No. Something went wrong. When he called me in because he was suspicious. And when he altered his will, because of the same suspicions.'

'Do you think so?'

'I think perhaps he told his murderer something he only suspected, but it was so close to the truth it was dangerous. And then he had to be killed.'

'Somewhere in all this there must have been a lot of money involved.'

'There still must be. And that brings in Touloupian.'

During the evening Joy tested out her own suspicion, which was that the school where little Touloupian and little Frowser had played football together, and a vicious game it must have been, would turn out to be the one where Dr Stoup had once been school chaplain. But that conjecture turned out to be mistaken. Still, Joy was consoled by fresh fish for supper. Saturday evening's catch, I suppose they ought to have been, but they tasted as fresh as if someone had spent Sunday out in the Channel. There isn't much left nowadays for someone of my age of what used to be the simple pleasures of life, but there is still fresh fish.

The Isle of Wight is a reviving and relaxing place to be. We thought over the situation again at night and discussed it again. With Saintly's suicide the urgency seemed to have drained away from what was happening. Unless the plot had now been put into reverse. We did mention that possibility, but only when we were both half asleep. We never took it seriously enough. We should have considered that Saintly was already trying to reverse the plot. He was not going to wait for any more elaborate hoaxes which might go wrong. He was coming straight down here to recover the material of the second excavation. It was already in place, but he was going to murder the vicar and recover that material alone.

We ought to have considered that once the material was in place, buried in Dr Stoup's mound on his building-site in the shadow of Carisbrooke, and once the initial hoax had gone sour, there was nothing left for the plotters to do but go into reverse. They could not risk ever producing the second dig, because it would link so clearly with the first. It would link them with Ralph Iggleby's altered will and his death. So they would make for the island as swiftly and as discreetly as possible, and open the mound secretly, if only to recover the very valuable treasures they had put in it. I do not know why we failed to realize this. Probably because we also failed to imagine the value and the grandeur of the phoney Greek treasure which lay on that night in the earth, at the vicar's building-site.

The Rev Dr Stoup came down on the Monday, but he was not left alone. Touloupian at least and perhaps others were already installed in the island. The time for trusting one another was over. It had gone out of the vicarage window with Doctor Saintly. What was done would have to be done together. They were like a political party with communal leadership. Biggleswade was not hanging about the grave-mound with his dog by chance. He was stationed there. Why did I not give my name as Ben Nevis or John Smith? Lack of forethought. But by the time Joy and I were sliding the fresh sole away from its bones, Touloupian knew, and the vicar very likely also knew, that Jonson and a girl had been snooping about the top of the downs and Jonson had investigated the mound.

Biggleswade was an employee, not a conspirator, otherwise I would never have got so much out of him; though I might have guessed most of what I did get. Biggleswade had been told there was trouble in the planning department, a double cross of some sort, and anyone whatsoever who approached the building-site or stopped to stare at it was to be questioned and reported. He knew nothing about the significance of the grave-mound except from the point of view of planning permission. Indeed, he could hardly have been told what lay underneath it. The temptation to excavate on his own would simply have been too great.

So when I sauntered out the next morning to sniff the air, I had not a thought in my head that anything was urgently wrong.

14

In the outside world nothing was stirring but an ordinary Monday morning. It was the sort of day when a routine takes over that seems to have lasted since childhood. Newport was not unlike the town streets of my childhood, the big dog on its own outside the butcher's shop, the bicycle and the shopping baskets and the superior town café and the bank. I had business to do in the bank, so I crossed over the road and went in. Something familiar about a man with his back to me. I bent over the counter to write my cheque.

When I had found my way back to the hotel the porter called me.

'There was a message for you, sir.'

'Who from?'

'Didn't say, sir. Said they'd ring back in ten minutes. I said you wouldn't be gone long. Your wife's just gone upstairs, sir.'

I thanked him and thought no more of it. When the phone rang upstairs I picked it up thoughtlessly.

'Police here, sir. Local police. That is Mr Jonson?'

'Yes it is.'

'We were wondering how you were getting on, sir. Like to keep our eye open.'

'Quite all right, thank you. Enjoying myself.'

'Good, sir. Glad to hear it. You haven't found out anything we ought to know about?'

'Not new to you, no.'

'How did you spend yesterday then, sir?'

Something clicked together in my mind. I had heard that voice before. A policeman who rang me up about Touloupian.

'Didn't I tell you last night?'

'Not us, sir. Not to my knowledge. What was it, sir?'

'Where are you speaking from?'

'Down in Cowes, sir. Cowes police station. What was it you wanted to tell us, sir?'

'About how I thought I was being followed. I could have sworn I spoke to you.'

'Not us, sir. Must have been some other station. It all comes through of course, but later in the morning.'

'You said you'd check on it. Or they did. Whoever I spoke to.'

'I see, sir. I expect that will be being acted on. I'm sure that's all right. Don't you worry about it. There was nothing else, was there, that we ought to know about?'

'No, nothing. I just walked about. I saw the vicar's building-plot.'

'Ah, well, keep in touch with us, then.'

'Yes of course. I'll be in Cowes later today. Shall I call in to see you?'

'No need for that, sir. No. I shall be out on patrol most of today.'

'I see. Thank you then.'

'Thank you, sir.'

I was as sure as I could be that the person on the other end of that line was not a policeman. None of it rang true. None of it at all. There was an easy way to find out, and I took it at once. I rang Cowes police station. No one had telephoned me. Neither from there nor from anywhere else so far as they knew. I was asked to go carefully through every detail of the call.

'There was something wrong, sir, which they thought you'd noticed. And they wanted to be sure if you'd told me. Just as well you didn't notice anything.'

'But I did.'

'What was that, sir?'

'A man called Biggleswade. Gooseberry eyes, not very tall. He has a big alsatian dog called Caesar. He was guarding Dr Stoup's building-site as if it was a gold mine. I came across it by chance, and it was just as I thought: it might be. It had an unexcavated grave-mound in the back garden.'

'What? No, a real one. Prehistoric.'

'No, it isn't a listed monument. It isn't even on the map.'

'Biggleswade. Yes. Said he was the agent.'

'I don't know if it was Joe Biggleswade. It could be.'

'Yes, brown and white check tweed, very loud. That's right.'

'Has he? What kind of record?'

'Oh I see.'

I was more infuriated than alarmed by having stumbled into what I felt were the loose ends of our exhausting week, but Joy, when I told her everything, was seriously frightened. If such a thing happened today, I would know that in those matters she is always right. At the time I smiled and shrugged and hoped for the best. We decided to spend the most placid day we could. We were due to return home on the Tuesday. I could not sit for ever on the Rev Dr Stoup's grave-mound like an Anglo-Saxon dragon guarding his hoard. Nothing it produced was likely to fool me now.

The placid day was to be spent at Osborne. Osborne Park lies to the east of Cowes harbour. No road passes along the coast.

The park is a solid royal estate stretching inland from the sea. The palace Queen Victoria built for herself has seen several uses in the eighty years since she died. At present most of it is open to the public. To say that its architecture is undistinguished is to put it too baldly. It has the air of a water works. It fills one with gloom. The furnishings are huge and royal and solemn. There was one splendid round table made of three hundred different kinds of wood, all inlaid into each other, one from every colony and dependency in the British Empire. I must confess that I liked that very much. But the effect of Osborne is overwhelming without gaiety.

Osborne dozes in its grounds. Huge trees sleep all round it. Dark shrubberies underlie the darker conifers. One could hear, as it were, 'only through the chestnut leaf the chestnut pattering to the ground'. In the right season. Now there was a heavy, sleepy smell of pine trees and the sea. Down the ridiculous parade grounds of mown grass we wandered, along path after path, through glade after glade, finding spring flowers. We came out on the shore at a small building designed by Prince Albert, a Palladian Tuscan farmhouse in miniature, with twin flights of steps and a boathouse underneath it. That was where Victoria used to give tea to Gladstone when he insisted on seeing her. She never invited him up to the palace. Maybe she was ashamed of it.

It was there that they found us. We were gazing out to sea when I heard footsteps on the path under the pine trees. I turned to see who was coming, because that afternoon we had most of the grounds of Osborne to ourselves. I was in time to see Touloupian. He was pointing, and before I could say a word he was gone again into the late-Victorian gloom.

Three tough-looking men were advancing on us. I yelled out to Joy, 'Run, see you later,' and took off fast in the opposite direction. Thank God it was not Joy they were after. That was what I hoped, but one of the men ran after her. She ran east and I ran west, then, seeing that was blocked, out to sea. It was a good enough idea. I am no runner but I can swim, and that boathouse can hardly be more than half a mile from the Medina river. The two tough-looking men just stood their ground and watched me.

What I had failed to reckon with was the extremely slippery cobble-stones just under the mud. I fell twice. The stones must have something to do with the old slipway. The two men advanced towards me. They did not fall. When I got up the second time, the bigger one said, 'You're making us trouble,' and knocked me down again into the sea. Then the smaller one came and fished me out and said, 'Fair's fair,' and just threw me a little way without hitting me. I landed on my face.

'Feel like running?' he said. 'Feel like a swim?'

'Making us trouble,' said his friend.

When they got me up the bank I thought I might try shouting, but the friends saw that coming.

'Here,' said the big one, 'hold 'im then.' And hit me again twice.

The smaller one, who had arms like a gorilla, said, 'Fair's fair, you 'old 'im.' He hit me only once, but that was the end of my day out. They had to carry me to the car. It stood idling at the end of the path; it was a groundsman's van. In the back of that I was wrapped in a rug and blindfolded and my arms and legs tied. It was a terribly uncomfortable journey. If Joy had got away there was some hope. She would go to the police. She would telephone from the palace. Did Queen Victoria have a telephone? At least Joy was not in this van. When I rolled over I got kicked in the ribs.

At last after a most bumpy bit of driving the van halted and I was dragged out of the back doors. This time I was being carried rather carefully. I could hear creaking. The slight slapping of water. For a nasty moment I thought I was being dumped in the river. I might not have drowned but I was still freezing cold from the sea. There was a smell of sea. There was no doubt that I was lying in the bottom of a boat. Someone told me to lie still, not that I had any choice really. The motor was an outboard motor. It was not a terribly long journey. We never crossed the Solent, I was sure of that. The Solent is a choppy few miles of water and I was in a mood to sympathize with Gladstone. This journey was smooth. The Medina river then, or one of the little inlets with private docks. Was there not an abandoned village in the west of the island with a beautiful empty customs house and an unused harbour? We must be somewhere like that.

Then I was being hauled up the side of a big dock. Was it a dock? Dumped hard on a wooden surface. Picked up like a baby and handed downwards. Dropped on a carpeted floor. Some kind of trapdoor slammmed behind me. There I lay for a time. Either I was still giddy or the floor was slowly, very gently heaving and shifting. Strange creaks from several directions. A yacht of course. Not a small one either. An ocean-going yacht with carpet in the saloon. I tried rolling over again but it taught me nothing. I waited until somebody came.

It was dark. They took off my blindfold and undid my ropes, and stood over me while I ate. Some sort of nauseating fry-up. Not nauseating to a healthy schoolboy. Nor to the friends I suppose. But I was feeling extremely delicate, and hurting in several places, including the mouth. Still, at least they contemptuously allowed me to walk a few steps up and down, and they brought me some dry clothes. So I was not going the way of Ralph Iggleby. I was just being kept out of harm's way for a time. How long? So I asked.

'How long am I here for?'

'Not long. Don't make us no trouble that's all.'

'Hours or days?'

'That depends on our boss; just you don't make no trouble and you'll be all right.'

'It's a mistake locking people up.'

'We haven't made no mistake.'

'Where's the girl?'

'Making us trouble, isn't she? Your doing isn't it?'

'How is it my doing?'

'Telling that girl to run. And now where is she?'

'How do I know?'

'You don't know, we don't know. Making trouble isn't it? We'll find her though. She won't get out of Osborne.'

'Who is your boss?'

'Put them on.'

'Who is he?'

'You know 'im don't you? You saw 'im didn't you? Being cunning are you? Want another doing over, do you?'

'Shall I thump 'im?'

'No, 'e's bin thumped enough, 'aven't you matey? Bin thumped silly, 'e 'as. Young Bill give 'im one.'

'Oh Gawd. Poor bugger.'

'What happens now?'

'Nothing don't happen now, do it?'

'I mean, when can I speak to your boss?'

'That's up to 'im, innit? Now remember, no trouble.'

And they left me for the night. But I knew now where I was. I knew it with some clarity. There were only five places like it left in the world. The size of the saloon, the dilapidated age of what was left of the fittings, and the elegance of its design left no doubt. I was somewhere I had always wanted to be. This was the rotting hull of a J-class racing yacht. It had to be a yacht, I thought: it was wood not metal, and it was huge. They raced in these before 1939, and when George V died they took his yacht out to sea and sank it off the Nore. These yachts had a crew of over thirty. These are the fastest and the most beautiful sailing boats ever built.

Or they once were. They were so delicate that when they raced, a shiver ran right through them from end to end. You felt it in every plank. They were millionaires' toys, even by the standards of those days. One of the last afloat was the *Atlantic*. She had a flush-riveted hull of quarter-inch iron plates. Her baths were marble with golden taps. She carried twelve stewards and her belaying pins were made of silver. But at sixteen knots she shivered all over, and she sailed so low in the water that she took ton after ton of sea over her lee deck. She was steered by two men lashed to twin wheels, relieved every half hour. When one of those J-class yachts had new sails fitted, it took a hundred men just to carry the new sail down Cowes High Street. They had fearful trouble getting it round the corners.

Now there are five left. Only the hulls are left, moored like barges or stuck on mudbanks. None of them can ever be reused as they were intended. It would cost too much. The sort of stripped-down little ocean racers they use today, *Morning Cloud* and her rivals, are nursery boats by comparison. The more I considered the proportions of the room I was in, the surer I became that I was inside one of those floating hulks.

What an illustrious way to drown. Because that looked like the next step. If anything at all went wrong, I would be got rid of. This was not an escape boat, whatever else it was. It was a hideout. It was a lair. A feature of the scenery that no one noticed because they had all known it for so long.

It would be mad to wait patiently. At the best, I was going to be left here alone when the friends had gone, and then I might escape or I might be discovered or not as the case might be. And my being allowed to survive at all assumed that Touloupian was intending to disappear from Britain altogether. Why should he do that? How could he market his treasures, real or false, without being followed up? Did he want to make a bargain with me? He was going the wrong way about it. Looking back now, I think he had simply not made up his mind.

He had to recover what was in the grave-mound. The vicar was arriving and they must work quickly or risk interference. If the police were convinced there was a serious reason for it, they would dig that mound themselves. And that is just what might have happened in the end. Once I had seen the mound and the fence and the tree-scars and the man with the alsatian and the criminal record, I would have gone home and convinced the inspector or the officer from London that this bizarre-sounding half-crime lay behind the murder of Ralph Iggleby. So of course Touloupian had to get me out of the way. I was doomed from the moment I spoke to Biggleswade. I was doomed from the moment I set foot on the island.

As for Joy, I had no idea where she might be, but I thought not on this hulk. I explored my position, feeling my way around the saloon. It had three portholes, one of them with some glass in it. There was no movable furniture. No nails or screws. Nothing like a weapon. If only I had my faithful hammer, I remember thinking. I scraped and pushed at this and that until I was near to tears. I had the carpet up but it revealed no trapdoor. Or did it? Flush with the floor. Square. Holes at the corners full of dirt. No way of lifting it.

I might be better employed putting my shoulder to the rotten hull. Not much use if this was a steel-built yacht. The square began to move. I had a comb. If only they had left me a fork from supper. Hard to lever up a trapdoor with a comb. Or a fork come to that. It was not a trapdoor though. It was more like the cover of a manhole, and I found the lifting-ring. Feeling about in the dark, I missed it, because it was flush with the floor. Then as I moved from one corner to another, my hand touched it.

I had to decide whether to use it or not. Suppose it led nowhere? I knew little about the bowels and the bilges of boats. Suppose that once having got down there I was unable to get up again? I had no light and almost none came through the portholes. I was not at all sure of the time. I had taken whatever was left from my pockets, but my watch was gone. There was no sound on the hulk, but was it safe to assume I was alone there? After the friends withdrew I had certainly heard a boat. But how many rooms were in use in the old hull? I knew from memory that there was nothing or virtually nothing left of any of the surviving yachts above the deck line. If any sentry had been posted, I ought to hear him moving about over my head. Or somewhere nearby, there would have been a light.

The only light I remembered had been a shaft of dim, rivery twilight from above. And I was surely quite close to the stern of the yacht. In fact to judge it by shape, which I paced out and fingered over again, this probably was the stern. I had certainly not been carried very far below decks when I was dumped here. I doubted if much of this yacht was usable at all. I was surprised to find my own quarters so dry. A steel hull I suppose. The more I pondered and hesitated, the more confident I became that the friends had left me alone on board. Someone would be watching, but only from the bank. In the front seat of the van, maybe.

I could find out by yelling. But that would surely mean another beating. For which I had no appetite, and as they say no stomach. What strange tricks the nervous system plays. My stomach began to ache and heave at the thought, and I felt the blood draining out of my face. There was no sense in hanging about and no point in taking risks. I picked at the ring until I got it upright. Then a heave. It stayed tight shut. It was awkward on the hands. I took off the woollen jersey the friends had brought me, and threaded its arms through the ring.

Several times I gave up to rest. Once I gave up altogether and wrapped myself in the carpet, but sleep was not possible for long, the whole ship stank of the river, and I went back to my task. Maybe if I had been successful sooner it would have been no use. By the time the cover shifted, dawn was breaking. Sedge warblers and sparrows and skylarks and woodlarks and wheatears and God knows what were tuning up in all directions. A grey gleam showed me whereabouts I was crouching on the floor. The cover came up, then it came away. It was a heavy brute of a thing.

The hole stank. It was surely below water level, and for all I knew it was flooded. I listened for the scurry of rats. Nothing came. Only a dripping noise in the distance. Where was the floor below me? There was no saying. I felt around, feebly stirring the air with my feet, holding myself with both elbows on the floor of the saloon. Then of course my feet found the ladder. I descended into a mysterious chamber. I think now it was a store for sails, but it was quite empty, curiously warm and bone-dry. It extended, as I found by trial and error, a long way forward. And incredibly, against all my inward feelings, which by now were despairing, I saw light.

It was as well there was light, because it gleamed on a lake of dark water. Something had smashed or rotted overhead, and the forward part of this chamber was flooded. An inch. No more than an inch or two of rainwater. Slimy underfoot but not impossible. Step by careful step I ventured forward. The question of the friends began to loom larger. But before that was settled I still had to negotiate a climb. Perhaps I might find another ladder, but in that darkness, among those heavy structures and in that long, long place I had little hope. I came to the point where the lower deck was open to the sky.

I could hardly have been luckier. There was some kind of loading bay, not very far above water level. Its door had rusted and twisted. Probably someone had tried to take it for scrap, or for a souvenir. Anyway it was at an easier height than the deck level of the saloon; I could easily reach it. The brown water was swirling past outside, about at the level of my feet. The hull was vast. I could see it stretching away forward, roughly painted up against the weather. It was possible now to make out colours. I had little time to lose.

What I first intended was to make my way back to the saloon, fetch my yesterday's wet clothes, replace the carpet and close the manhole cover over my head. It would win me a little time perhaps. The friends had shown more muscle-power than intelligence. My cunning carefulness might delay them five minutes. But when I looked back, the darkness was intense. The old ship creaked gently. I was shivering with fear. I needed to get away now, to get right away, to get far beyond pursuit. I would go with the tide, whichever way it was moving.

I wondered for a minute or two how bare to strip, but after all even wet clothes are better than none, and men in wet clothes are not unheard of in the streets of Cowes. Anyway I needed my pockets. Besides, I was still aching from yesterday, still cold and shivering, and still afraid. Clothes are some comfort. I was not looking forward to my morning's swim. So here goes. It occurred to me I had little idea how deep the water was. Then I was in it, going as fast as I could underwater along the side of the hull. I came up for a last long breath under the shadow of the great bows. So far I had hardly made more disturbance than a waterbird might make. It was terribly cold in the river, and the wind was icy.

My clothes had kept me from the first shock of the cold but as they soaked and grew heavy it was the coldness more than their weight that got to me. I disappeared under the surface and travelled as far as I could downstream. The aim was to reappear not at the opposite bank, which was tempting, and not close in to the reeds of the near bank either, but just as far away as I could get in midstream. The friends had a boat, and probably a good view downstream and downtide. All I could hope for was not be be noticed or recognized. I surfaced for not much longer than a salmon does.

The signs were, as I discovered later, that the friends really had left a sentry on deck. He had smoked away the night there. But the moment of daybreak is distracting. Maybe he had been watching the fields, waiting for a relief. 'Fair's fair,' perhaps he was saying. But he never saw me, and I never saw him. By the second or third time I surfaced, the old hulk was indistinguishable from a distant barge. There was no pursuit and no sign of life. I splashed across to the opposite bank. I seemed to be in someone's back garden. There was a canoe with paddles lying there. Should I have taken it?

I wanted to get right away from the river, and a house means a road, so I soon found my way dripping and squelching and shivering into the suburbs of Cowes. I tried to run but all I could manage was a lame, staggering movement no faster than a walk. The first thing was to try to find Joy. I rang the hotel, reversed charges. They were reluctant to accept that, but when I explained I had had a boating accident they became pleasanter. At last I got the manager.

'No sir. She is not in the hotel.'

'No, we wondered where you both were, sir. I hope the accident was nothing serious?'

'No sir, we might have informed the police this morning. But when we found the car back in the yard last night...'

'Yes sir, about nine last night.'

'Thank you, sir.'

My next move was obviously to find the police. Not much sense in telephoning, but I did so just for form. A patrol car came whizzing round the corner within two minutes.

15

The Cowes police wanted immediate action. A masterful elderly officer with a bald head began marshalling his forces before I stopped talking. I had the impression that old-fashioned bruisers like the friends are rarer now than they used to be. In my view they ought to be preserved like an endangered species in some sort of human zoo. Dartmoor would do nicely. The police seemed to have even stronger feelings, these men not being Isle of Wighters.

'They're not from the island. Not them. Else they'd know more about those hulls. Ought to know that wouldn't be secure.'

'Were they armed?'

'At no time?'

'No threat of shooting? The guard wasn't armed?'

'He didn't need to be.'

'And this Touloupian. London man is he?'

'He has a shop there certainly. He seems to be an Armenian with Egyptian connections.'

'Gawd. Are the others London men?'

'Well, I should say so by the accent. But you can't tell so easily now, can you?'

'No you can't. Same accent from Hastings to Hertfordshire. Including Southampton. So you can't place them or describe them?'

'Not very clearly. Dark hair. Strong. They looked like fairground people. Something like that. Or dockers.'

'Well, let's take a look at them, shall we, sir? If you don't mind coming along with us? Just to identify. You will recognize them?'

'Oh yes. I will recognize them.'

We sped away in a comfortable police car, with other cars ahead of us. By the time we got close to the river, policemen seemed to be in position in every hedge. It was a very smooth action. They had the riverside sealed off on both sides of the river, and a launch on the river itself.

'Now we'll flush them out,' said the bald-headed officer. He spoke a few words to a radio. The radio spluttered a reply.

I could hear the launch hailing the hulk. Then a long silence. The police would be going aboard. A long, long silence. The radio spluttered again.

'He says it's empty, sir. There have been people there. There's a galley with dirty plates, yesterday's grease. Everything as you described it. No sign of the girl. No sign she was ever there. They're bringing your clothes. And they found your watch. Smashed, I'm afraid that is, with the galley poker. Last thing they did, I dare say, when they found you gone. Hullo?' The radio was crackling like an electric storm.

'Ah yes. I dare say. Says they left traces all over the place, sir. We shall have them then. Sooner or later. Run as they like.'

'Have they got away?'

'Oh yes, sir. They'll be away out of the island by now.

They're gone all right. There was one of them on deck most of the night. We shall have him described by someone before the day's out. And this groundsman's van, sir, can you describe it?'

No one in my condition when I saw it could possibly have described it. I admitted as much and the officer surveyed me gloomily.

'Never mind, sir, what you need now is some breakfast, and a rest. We'll give you breakfast at the station, and then we'll leave you at your hotel.'

'Oh I can get my own breakfast.'

'Not at this hour. Not out of season. Not in the Isle of Wight.'

It was still not half past seven in the morning.

'And what about Joy?'

'They won't have taken her, sir. I doubt that. If she ever got caught at all.'

'She'd have come to you if she wasn't caught.'

'She ought to have done, sir, I agree. But she may turn up yet. I'm sure we shall find her. The day's early yet. She may turn up, sir, you may find. May have been scared, may have hidden up somewhere, spent the night, you can't tell. May have left the island. I'm sure you'll hear from her. Your wife is it, sir?'

'No. Wish she was.'

'Ah, quite, yes, ah. Ah yes indeed sir. Well I hope she turns up all the same sir. We shall be working on it. I shall have men over at Osborne this morning, sir.'

'There was one more thing.'

'And what was that, sir? Here we are in Cowes then. If you'll step this way we can soon find breakfast in the canteen. This way.'

'One more thing. About Touloupian.'

'Ah yes, they'll be running him through the computer this morning, sir.'

'Haven't they done that yet?'

'Not to my knowledge, sir. Of course that's the central police computer. Costs a million pounds a minute. But it's far more efficient than the old-fashioned records.'

'Oh yes sir. Oh yes indeed. You take those two you call the friends. You'd have found them in the old records.

Fingerprints, usual behaviour, build, previous convictions, known associates. You'd have found all that in a day or two. By the time we've eaten this breakfast sir, they'll be in the queue. And later this morning we shall know everything about them. Even without prints, we should know how many old-fashioned villains are loose like that who might take this job. We'd know who had any connections here, in the island. We'd know where to look for them when they hid.'

I knew that it was true. There was recently a Chief of Anti-terrorist Police in West Germany who concentrated on computers. One of the things he found out was that terrorists move around. They take extraordinary safety precautions. They never have a garage where you'd expect it. They never introduce their friends to their neighbours. Now it so happens that most, almost all West Germans settle their electricity bills by cheque or some equivalent of a postal order. That anchors their name, with all the information about credit and money and taxes that attaches to a name nowadays, to the use of electricity and the premises. It occurred to this German policeman that a terrorist would pay in cash. That knowledge came out of a computer. So he ran through everyone in West Germany who payed cash for electricity. He investigated them all. Of the last two that he failed to eliminate in other ways, one turned out to be a member of the Baader-Meinhoff gang. Of course, some would say that the Germans exaggerate in these matters. All I can say is that I hope to have them on my side in the next world civil war.

'I thought we ought to look at that mound.'

'What mound?'

'On the Rev Dr Stoup's building-land. The grave-mound I visited. The reason they came and got me I suppose.'

'Yes sir, that might be wise. You would recognize if it had been disturbed?'

He had more faith in computers than in the human observers whose records are fed into them. Rightly I suppose, because the records have been double-checked, and any contradiction produces red lights and mechanical indigestion at once.

Before we left I was told that Touloupian's name and characteristics had been fed into the infernal machine. He had no criminal record of course. What he did have was tax problems. He was thought to keep three sets of books, like an old uncle of mine, one to show profit for partners and associates, one to show loss for the tax lawyers, and the third hand-written in a very small, tattered notebook that seldom left his inside pocket. That told the truth, it was thought, but no one else had ever seen it. Touloupian showed up badly only through his associates. The associates' record is the most crippling weapon of the police computer.

Statistics tell the truth a given percentage of times. One can even know that number of times, that is the precise degree of credibility of each conclusion from the evidence. When these circles of associates coincide, when the same innocent name crops up too often, the likelihood increases by exact mathematical proportions that the name, which in the old days might have escaped any close enquiry, is worth a serious investigation. What used to be dismissed in that shadowy category, 'known associate of criminals', which might be true of anyone, certainly of any policeman, can now be instantly correlated with other factors. The number of times that his car was recorded near the scene of a crime. His financial situation. And so on.

Touloupian's known associates had been regrettable on more than one occasion. The suspicion arose that he was a friend and employer of thieves, even possibly a fence. He certainly spent a lot, and his money troubles had increased recently. 'Like everyone's,' sighed the old policeman, 'things being as they are.' His residences were listed, but none on the Isle of Wight. His journeys abroad went far beyond Egypt. He had an American partner. The most interesting thing about him from my point of view was his attendance at a Congress for the Study of Techniques in Prehistoric Jewellery. That was listed only as the reason for a journey abroad. There was no information about his origins, which I supposed was to be expected. Indeed I was rather glad. I am not sure that I like computers.

We drove up through Newport to the building-site. It was quite undisturbed. Mr Biggleswade and his alsatian dog had vanished like the baseless fabric of a dream. Since I still thought then that the trick with the antiquities lay in the uncharted future, I was satisfied. I did suggest that the police might keep an eye on it. They did agree that they would. There was no point in setting a guard. The old officer, whose appetite for work was undiminished, thought he might go and call on Joe Biggleswade. Not to take him in, because there was nothing against him now, even though he had a record. He had not been the third man in the grounds of Osborne. He had never appeared on the hull of the *Clover*, the old J-class ocean yacht. He had not been doing more than his job. There was just a faint hope he might lead to Touloupian. Or to Joy.

I was in despair about Joy. If she were free she would surely race for the hotel, or for the police. When I got in at the hotel I telephoned Winchester and Stonehouses, and home. There was no news of her. I went down and examined the car. She had left no message there, no trace of herself. The last thing I thought of doing was telephoning to Murray's, in Cowes High Street. When I shouted out to her yesterday, 'See you later,' that was what I meant. We had been planning to have dinner there last night. It was new to both of us, but its outside aspect suited us, and it was our day off. We were getting to know each other, just wandering about. Passion may teach you a lot, and any strange adventure gives you a sense of fellow-feeling. But just wandering about together is the way to know somebody.

'I was ringing about last night's table. My name is Jonson. I'm afraid I booked a table but I was unable to come and claim it. And I couldn't phone.'

'It's kind of you to phone now at least, Mr Jonson.'

'No. I'm really sorry. The girl never came I suppose?'

'Hold on now. The girl? Oh yes, there was . . . what name was it?'

'Jonson. Did she leave a message?'

'No, I don't think so. No. But the table was taken.'

'A girl with freckles?'

'Yes, she had freckles.'

'Very pretty?'

'Quite striking, yes.'

'She came?'

'Oh yes.'

'What happened? What time was it?'

'Early. We open the bar early, and she sat a long time.'

'Alone?'

'Oh yes, quite alone.'

'When did she leave?'

'Oh quite late. And she booked the same table.'

'She did?'

'Yes, in the same name. Jonson. For tonight. You're in luck Mr Jonson.'

'Yes I am. Yes, I am indeed. I'll see you tonight then.'

'Very well, Mr Jonson. We'll see you tonight.'

I flung myself down on the bed. I was aching. I had hardly the energy to move. I took my clothes off somehow, singing myself an endless ballad to keep myself awake. Did I dare take a bath or would I fall asleep in it? I ran it and fell asleep in it. Half dried. Crashed into bed and slept until mid-afternoon.

I was woken by a dream. In my dream we were in a boat, sliding over a snow-cold waterfall.

'Move over a bit,' she said.

She was really there.

'Are you all right?'

'Are you all right?'

'Mm.'

'Mm.'

'Glad to see you.'

'Glad to see you.'

We slept another two hours. When I woke it was still true. There were her things daintly scattered. There were mine in an unwieldy pile. There she was, as secure as anything on this earth, sweetly slumbering beside me, with one arm outstretched.

It will not take long to supply her missing day from her point of view. There is no sense in recording how she told the story, because thrilled as I was to get her back in one piece, I kept interrupting. We had a bottle of cold fizzy wine and tea and cucumber sandwiches. Then at the same time she was questioning me. I had a mark on my face which came in for attention, and another on my ribs. Come to think of it I must have been an alarming sight, in spite of my bath. She was as pretty as a picture.

What had happened was this. Joy raced off to the east, away

from Cowes, into a dense thicket of trees. The man who followed her dashed into the thicket close behind her, but luckily for Joy she came on a path at once, and better still, it divided. She shouted then, though I never heard her: her idea was to work her way round to where I was. I am ashamed to say she thought I could dispose of my two men. But he headed her off, and the crashing through the bushes suddenly ended with Joy bursting out on to the vast lap of the Victorian lawn. The house stands a little way inland, and it looked like a straight race. But she noticed the bruiser sheering away to the right, towards a van. It occurred to her that he might pursue her in that. She was still some way from the house.

There in front of her was a children's football game. No adult, no one she could tell, and the children were quite small. But there were seven or eight of them and she was in fear of her life, so she asked if she could join in. And they let her. If I were to approach a children's football game like that, I'd be arrested for improper advances. But Joy is a pretty, fresh-faced girl like all their mothers and sisters. Of course they let her join in. All the bruiser could do was hang about and watch. By the time the kids got tired of football, Joy was their best friend. They all left together, in a tight group.

I never saw them, but Joy saw me carried into the van, and she took the van's number. She still went on playing. The man who was after her must have felt a fool. The children were local, and he slunk along behind her in the street as they dropped away. But the gate of Osborne is in the suburbs of East Cowes. East Cowes is nothing but a suburb really: a suburb and a landing-place. It was so public he must either lose her, which seeing she had the van number he dared not do, or attack her and get arrested, or do what he did do. He followed close enough behind to catch her if she ever made a false move, but far enough away to escape if she ever screamed for a policeman.

She did want to get to the police, but she was obsessed with what might happen to me. He'd come close enough to her to say something about that, as they crossed over the Medina river into West Cowes. He told her to come with him or else it would be the worse for me. She pretended she hadn't heard, and tried to put a distance between them, but of course she brooded on it and half believed it. She tried hard to shake him off, but how? There are not many buses, and if she got on one so would he. Her safest plan was to stay in crowded places all day. That was what she did.

She hoped that in the end he would give up and set off for home, for wherever the others were. Then she would follow him. The pursuer pursued. It might have worked too, if he'd been as stupid as my two friends. But he was the bright one of the three. Maybe that was why he chose the girl and left them the rough stuff. And she made one mistake. She stopped and had tea in a crowded tea shop, thinking what to do next and how to get a message to the police. She thought there must be a way if she could only think of it. But that gave him the opportunity to make a phone call. She saw him do it. And after that he followed her really closely.

She was exhausted by six. It was a ghastly thing to go through. No girl likes being watched or followed by a tough-looking man with some sort of physical designs on her. I'm sure there are other girls who might have treated her situation in different ways. She said so herself. She might have slammed him on the ear with a handbag and just screamed. He would probably have been arrested. But she was worried for me, and she dared not try anything that wasn't absolutely bound to work. So at half past six she went along to Murray's and sat there at the bar, wondering how to get the police a message he wouldn't intercept. He sat at the other end of the bar sucking up whisky. She waited and waited for me, in case I came.

What Joy went through was a nightmare in this aspect also, that everything since Osborne seemed to be happening to her in slow motion. In reality I was only a mile away, but she thought I might be at the bottom of the sea. What happened to me left me some small room for action, and it happened fast. If I have learned one thing in life it has been this. Hope in every sphere of life is a privilege that attaches to action. No action, no hope. On the other hand I have a friend who was once put through a course by the Royal Marine Commandoes. His sergeant used to tell these young men, 'While you've got boots and he's got balls, there's still hope.'

127

The time came when Joy had to leave Murray's. With amazing faithful loving loyalty she booked a table for the same time tomorrow, that is another rendezvous with me, in case I could make it. Before she left, she visited the Ladies, and there, behind the mirror, she left a message to the police that was bound to reach them next morning if not before. Alas, the cleaning lady thought it was some drunken joke and tore it up unread. Then Joy ordered a taxi by telephone. Of course her follower did the same. He also probably had her taxi cut off at the hotel. She never would have got indoors. But the hours and hours of munching salmon mousse and fresh lobster had given her a breathing-space, and she thought of something brilliant.

Her taxi drove her straight to the girls' school. It was nicely timed too. The girls were in bed but not the staff. Lights on everywhere. Her bruiser never even followed her in there. Probably never even guessed where she went. Miss Stoup put her up for the night. The one thing she asked her in return was to do nothing the next morning until Miss Stoup had reassured herself on what she called some personal aspects of this sad business. Perhaps she meant that she had to talk to her brother, who was in the building by then. But the brother got up late or the conversation took a long time. She gave Joy lunch and packed her off in another taxi to see the police. She said that in the circumstances she preferred not to have any more police in the school buildings.

You can see her point.

16

At this time a lot of things were happening at once. The police machinery was grinding steadily along. Touloupian's London shop was shut. It contained drawers full of unpaid bills. The friends were lying low, and Joy's follower, whose photograph was already on record, had been identified as a young thug last heard of in Brighton. That was where the police would start looking for him. The number of the van was less productive. It had been stolen a week ago in South London. The number plate would be different by now, or the van would be found abandoned. Easy come, easy go. Nothing more had emerged at Stonehouses, except that the police there had failed to persuade the Prouters to lodge their archaeological treasures in a bank. The owner of the *Clover,* the hulk where I had been imprisoned, had turned out quite innocent. There was still no trace of Touloupian.

It was Joy who discovered a small, valuable nugget of information about Touloupian. It had come from old Miss Stoup. She had spoken of her brother's literary friend Frowser, and his archaeological friend Tanner. The two boys had been at school on the island, at the school she mentioned before. Touloupian? Oh no, not a name like that. It was quite an ordinary school. Tanner, that was it. A small preparatory school for local boys. From which they went on, she fancied, to schools in the lower middle of the range of public schools on the mainland. She was sure Tanner and Touloupian could not be the same person.

It was worth telling the police, and lucky that we did so. Tanner had a quite different record from Touloupian but they overlapped. They had some of the same friends. And Tanner had gone to prison as a fence. Little was known but much more suspected. They had lived with the same woman. They were the same person without a doubt. Tanner had served his sentence and apparently gone straight. He had then quietly transformed himself into the Armenian with Egyptian connections. Frowser knew Tanner's secret, as he knew other secrets. As for the gap in the computer's knowledge, in the basic ability to connect, a computer can answer only the questions you ask it. No one had asked about a possible alias of Touloupian.

I had the curiosity now to ask old Miss Stoup and her brother much more about the young Tanner. I might even learn something from the venerable cleric about the grave-mound that he nourished in his back garden. It was after all an innocent subject, and it was out in the open now. It would even be rather close of me not to enquire about it. We called at about six, by appointment. We were formidably received with two glittering decanters of sherry by a line-up of the two Stoups and Miss Saintly, her nose in the air but her eyes a little wild. She smelt strongly of scent. To drown the smell of gin which was on her breath? It was possible, and none of my business.

We got through some frosty preliminaries.

'Ah so. Ah so,' intoned the vicar. 'The hero. The soldier's painter's scholar's eye, tongue, sword,' he observed wildly.

'The chiasmus, Alfred, does not encompass Mr Jonson,' said his sister.

'Eye yes, and tongue certainly. But you are not a soldier, Mr Jonson?'

'No, certainly not.'

'Nor a policeman? Though that would be the baton.'

'No.'

'Exactly not. Mr Justice Melford Stevenson lived at a house called Batons. Or was it Truncheons? I always thought that appropriate, whoever named it.'

'I have no doubt Alfreda that he built it himself. As I shall do my humble house.'

'What will you call yours, sir?' I asked him.

'Mount Ephraim? I think Mount Ephraim.'

'After...?'

'After the old tune. Ah, so, I see you love it too. The psalms are not sung as they used to be.'

'How used they to be sung?' asked Joy.

'Rolled,' put in Miss Stoup firmly. 'They rolled the psalm to wintery skies. Is that not true, Alfred?'

'Of the past, Alfreda, it may be. Of the remote past. But I referred to our childhood, a more comforting time.'

'A stricter time, Alfred, than these days. Worse in many ways, but stricter. A time of severe principles.'

'I am comforted by the name of Mount Ephraim. It shall be the name of my house.'

'That is a new decision, Alfred.'

'It is a new house, my dear.'

'It was to be called the Mound.'

'And now Mount Ephraim. So. A transformation.'

'About the mound, sir...'

'The mound?'

'Where you cleared the trees.'

'Ah yes. You have seen it. So.'

'A grave-mound I suppose.'

'And so I think. So indeed. So.'

'Late Bronze Age, it might be, or early Iron Age?'

'I shall baptize it Mount Ephraim. And that will be the end of the matter.'

'You intend keeping it?'

'Oh yes. For ever. No excavation for me. Not at all.'

'It will stay as it is when you make the garden? Forgive me, I can't bear not to ask, being an archaeologist.'

'It will be my idea of a wild garden. It shall remain undisturbed.'

'As a monument?'

'To the dead.' The vicar bowed his eccentric head and shook his ears like a donkey in a field.

Miss Saintly looked up at the ceiling and drank the rest of her sherry. Miss Stoup promptly offered us all some more.

'And shall you stay long in the island?'

'Not as long as we should like. A few more days maybe.'

'It is a peaceful island. I call it almost a holy island.'

'It has interesting Christian monuments? I wish I knew more about them.'

'That also. But my brother and I are not ashamed, are we Alfred? to imagine that some sanctity attaches to poetry. Do you believe that, Joy?'

'Er yes, I suppose I do, Miss Stoup.'

'I have heard Mr Jonson quote Shakespeare,' chanted the vicar with a certain irony. And a devilish sharp memory.

'This is an island of poetry,' she chanted back at him. 'I have always thought *The Tempest* was written after a visit to the Isle of Wight.'

'And there's Tennyson of course,' I murmured dutifully.

'After whom my brother was christened Alfred, and I Alfreda. And the young Keats at Shanklin. And Swinburne's house at Bonchurch and his grave.'

They were all drinking more sherry than was good for them.

'The romance of Carisbrooke,' added Miss Saintly, who

clearly knew this conversation by heart. 'The martyred king and his imprisoned daughter.'

The vicar was grimacing like a man with a raw carrot in his mouth.

'The dead,' he muttered.

'I can add to the list of poets,' I said brightly. The two ladies gave me sharp looks. 'Edward Lear came here to stay with Tennyson. He played Tennyson settings of his own poems on his piano. Julia Cameron the photographer lived at the bottom of Tennyson's drive. When she saw Lear coming she sent up her own piano carried by workmen. Where are those settings now, I wonder?'

'Had Tennyson no piano?' asked Miss Stoup coldly.

'I never heard that story,' said Miss Saintly most doubtfully.

'Would it not be a liberty?' asked the vicar. 'A piano is an expensive gift. Hm. And one wonders about the number of workmen.'

I leave it to the reader. My problem was that I hardly knew how to raise the subject of Tanner or Touloupian. Indeed in the end I funked raising it at all. It was Joy who tranquilly planted the barb.

'Do tell me, vicar,' she said, 'about your archaeological friend Tanner.'

'Tanner? You know Tanner?'

'We know him as Touloupian.'

'Ah indeed. A business name.

Slowly comes a hungry people, as a lion creeping nigher
Glares at one that nods and winks behind a slowly dying fire.'

He beamed mischievously, as if the question had been sufficiently answered.

But Miss Stoup continued. 'Mr Tanner is not a hungry people, nor are we nodding and winking over a dying fire. I do not see the analogy, Alfred.'

'I meant the name, Alfreda. *Nominis umbra*. It was the image that he wished to project.'

'Have you known him a long time?'

'Many years. Many years indeed.'

'Did you know he was in the Isle of Wight?'

'Tanner? Touloupian? In the island. Ah, it could be so. Indeed I had thought it might be so. Or I had thought he might have quite other business.'

'He is wanted by the police. They want to see him.'

'Ah so. These events have been shocking. We have had enough of them.'

'What will he do?'

'He will flit, like a shadow. *Nominis umbra*, as I said. There will reappear in Ohio a Mr Tombs, in Buenos Aires a Professor Taphopoulos, in Australia a Doctor Graves. It will have been prepared.'

'It is not decent,' said his sister, 'and it is not honest.'

'Not at all honest, Alfreda. Not at all. And the young girl will disappear also. Katya, whom you will have met in Bowen's shop.' The vicar gazed at me serenely as if we had already discussed Katya. The truth was that she had dropped right out of my mind. The revelation of her importance to Touloupian, of her having any importance at all, was a surprise to me. Nor did I know why the Rev Dr Stoup had let her name drop. I knew only that he was in control of himself.

'Poor Tanner,' he went on, 'has not been successful in life. He is young enough to start again.'

His sister burst out with some more Tennyson.

'Or to burst all links of habit – there to wander far away,
On from island unto island at the gateways of the day,
Larger constellations burning, yellow moons and happy skies.'

'Alfreda, the moons I think are mellow, not yellow. Does anyone remember?'

'Mellow moons and happy skies. You are right, Alfred. But the point is to burst the links of habit. That is what I meant. That is what Mr Tanner ought to do.'

'Habit, Miss Stoup?'

'The bad and ingrained habits of half a lifetime, Mr Jonson.'

I was at sea in this moralizing atmosphere, where lines of poetry were flung at one like the sea's waves. It seemed unlikely we were going to extract any further information from the vicar. Miss Saintly was dozing. Miss Stoup looked at her watch. I made one more attempt as we left.

'And the girl Katya, Miss Stoup; do you know anything about her?'

'She was a pupil here, years ago. I regret to say that she was a foolish girl, a bad pupil. We had in the end to part company. We expelled her. That is a grave step to take.'

'May I ask what for, Miss Stoup?'

'Let me show you out. We will leave Roberta Saintly here. She seems to be asleep. She needs to sleep. She ought perhaps to go away, but where? A clinic, do you think? She will be better here.'

'Thank you, Miss Stoup. That is Joy's coat. Thank you, vicar.'

They were hovering in the hall as we left.

'Mr Jonson, I was about to tell you how Katya came to be expelled.'

'Alfreda, is that not a personal secret? A privileged piece of knowledge? She was young at that time.'

'On the contrary it is something it may be useful to Mr Jonson to know. And of its nature it is better it should be public. She attempted to blackmail poor Roberta Saintly.'

'Is not blackmail too hard a word, Alfreda?'

'It is exact. She attempted to blackmail Roberta Saintly, about gin. Roberta had the common sense on that occasion to come to me at once. She is not well.'

'I hope, Alfreda, you have done no harm by confiding in Mr Jonson. I hope if he should encounter Katya again, he will always be discreet.'

I said of course. Of course I would be. Though my brain was already racing. Still, I could not see any essential role for Katya in Ralph Iggleby's violent death, or even in the confused circumstances of his last excavation. I wondered how or where I might encounter her again. Neither I nor anyone else was going to encounter her, had I only known it.

We telephoned the police from Murray's while the soles were grilling. Thirty years ago or more the best Channel sole used to be caught in the straits. The best plain fish restaurant, where perfect fresh fish was perfectly simply cooked, used to be on the waterfront at Ostend in those days. I remember the swifts and swallows twittering and screaming over narrow streets, but nothing else about Ostend except the heat of the evening and the quality of the fish. That is the kind of fish you could still get last year in Cowes, a few doors from the birthplace of Thomas Arnold, of all people. Does that make Matthew Arnold another Isle of Wight poet, I wondered? Matthew Arnold belongs to the ruined landscape around Oxford, always half imaginary in his poems, now quite imaginary. Or Matthew Arnold belongs to Dover cliffs. The beach is not what it was, and there are no Dover sole in Dover.

The police were very interested in Katya, and went to work at once to add her to the wanted list. Two people together are easier to trace than one alone, and very much harder to disguise. I reported the conversation with the Stoups as accurately as I could, but it was a dazing, allusive conversation even at the time, and sherry is a more intoxicating drink than one realizes, particularly on an empty stomach. The police had nothing more to report about Touloupian. His photograph was now being circulated, and tomorrow it would be published. They thought it improbable Joy and I had anything to fear, but they were watching Murray's and watching our hotel. We might do best, they suggested, to go home to Oxfordshire quite soon. I agreed. So long as someone kept an eye on that mound.

The evening passed easily and we began to relax again. No one followed us or disturbed us. When we went outside to the car, a constable wished us goodnight in a gruff, cheerful voice, and the same thing happened in Newport at the door of our hotel.

'At any minute,' said Joy, 'someone is going to call out eleven o'clock and all's well on a fine, clear night.'

'Well and so it is,' I said. But it was not.

135

17

The morning came, a little colder than before, and Joy and I had snuggled in our blankets for a long time. We had hardly taken the serious decision to get out of bed when the phone started ringing. It was the distant voice of the Oxford police.

'Mr Jonson?'

'Yes. Jonson here. Who is it?'

'This is the police, sir. From Oxford. We got your number from the local men, sir. They'll be along to interview you in a little while on our behalf.'

'What about?'

'A burglary, sir, at the Deer Park at Stonehouses.'

'Is it serious?'

'Yes sir, I'm afraid it is. They knew what they wanted and they took it.'

'Was anyone hurt?'

'Captain Prouter slept through it like a lamb. And Mrs Prouter says she may have heard something, but she never stirred.'

'Was it the archaeological material?'

'That's it, sir. You've put your finger on it. Captain Prouter was advised by us to have it locked away, but he wouldn't do it. Now sir, we haven't even an inventory of what was taken. Shall you be able to help us with that, sir?'

It had been a professional job. The police were furious with Prouter and Prouter was furious with me, for whose sake he claimed he had kept 'this stuff' available for study. The police could not possibly put a permanent or even a temporary guard on every entrance to the park or the house. The thieves had driven up in a car, parked it on the lawn, opened the library window, and cleared out everything from the archaeological cupboard. They had taken a few more things also: a rug that hung on the wall, some candlesticks and an oriental silver beaker. They took nothing of any importance because nothing of importance was left to take. Stripping the room of a few ornaments was only a token. I admit that I was relieved to have an alibi for the time of the crime. Captain Prouter had hinted to the police that I was a dark horse.

It was easy enough to supply an inventory of what came out of the Hallstatt grave. After several attempts, I even produced a reasonable drawing from memory of the gold bowl; I remembered its simple ornamentation, of which I now felt suspicious. The cows with suckling calves on the cauldron rim were much easier to deal with, because I knew where to find recently published photographs of very similar figures. And was there not something special, something that had been nagging me, about the way they were fixed to the brim? I was surprised that the crude local pottery had been taken. That might mean that the thief was not the mastermind of the operation. He had been told to take everything, including what was of no value.

Or was the intention not chiefly theft? Was it maybe to leave no hard evidence available at all of what Ralph Iggleby had dug up? If someone was now replanning the coup, leaving out the two digs that guaranteed each other and disposing of the most valuable material directly, then the existence of the earlier group of objects with mystery and doubt attaching to them would be an embarrassment. He would fear that I might at any time publish Ralph Iggleby's material, with a note on the circumstances. Suppose that I saw something wrong. That would at once cast doubt on any similar tomb-group, particularly on one closely connected to the first by so many coincidences of personality. By relationship of blood. By murder and by suicide.

It was only then that I half realized how probable it was that the whole plot was being put into reverse. Touloupian's problem was to withdraw the material he had hazarded. When it was uncovered as the grave-goods of an ancient king, it would have been worth millions. Perhaps literally millions of pounds. But even when he seeded it into the earth, it would represent a lot of money. There might easily be gold, and that would have to be genuine gold. Only its antiquity would not be genuine. Touloupian had taken back the grave-goods from Stonehouses because they no longer had a function. He would break them up, remodel them, sell them off very quietly.

And the Rev Dr Stoup had spoken of never digging up his mound. He had spoken about it with a weird passion. Perhaps he had been used by Touloupian (I could not accustom myself to calling him Tanner), just as he was used by the doctor. And what was the psychological key to that mysterious family? There was too much in common between Alfred and Alfreda for the suspicion to be absent that they were profoundly and irrationally linked. Why had Alfred become a clergyman? Was a severe and nursery Christianity not more essential to Miss Stoup than to her brother? Was it a quarrel, and a difference over religion, that was their deepest link? That is possible between brother and sister. They embrace the quarrel because somehow it locks them closer together. It excludes the rest of the world, as the habit of quoting Tennyson also might be designed to exclude it. Miss Stoup I believed to be protective and severe, with fits of a formidable realism. Roberta Saintly had opted out; she was no one's reliable ally.

And the vicar? The vicar was an alarming man. I was frightened of him and frightened for him. I had no way of measuring how close he was to Touloupian.

The telephone rang again and it was the police again. This time from London. This time the news was thrilling. In the course of checking on the girl Katya they had found, as we expected, that she had disappeared a few days ago, when the shop closed and her job ended. But she had vanished in a strange way. The office at Bowen's yielded her home address, which was a house in Fulham, the sort of small house where within living memory the families of domestic cleaning ladies used to live, now the height of impoverished fashion and smartness. When the police got to the house that morning, they found she had apparently been gone three days, but without stopping her milk or newspapers. Inside, the bright purple paint on the staircase was battle-scarred, the mobile in the hall was smashed, the bird's-nest wallpaper in the living room was ink-stained. The house had been burgled, thoroughly searched and smashed up.

The catastrophe must have occurred almost at once, because

since then two mornings' mail had piled up in the hall. Burglaries are sufficiently common in London for this one to be dismissed as a coincidence. People who advertise their absence with milk bottles and newspapers deserve what they get, or so I have heard it is said, both by criminals and by the police. But in Katya's case the obvious inference was that she had gone away with Touloupian. Touloupian himself had vanished as smoothly as a snowflake in a swimming-bath. Would he not take more care of Katya's disappearance? And she had left a lot of things behind, the treasures of girls of her generation and often their only riches: new pairs of tights, a gold plastic belt, high-heeled shoes and Elizabeth David cookery books.

The police had telephoned me about some photographs they found in a self-addressed envelope on the hall floor. It had just been delivered when the police arrived. They saw the postman driving away. So if this envelope had been due to be intercepted, the police, for almost the first time in this whole tangle of cases, were one move ahead. They sounded really pleased about it too. I would know of course, they suggested cautiously, that blackmailers did at times use the device of self-addressed letters? And there was, wasn't there, a history of blackmail? I had said that. More than most crimes, it was one that once committed was repeated. That and poisoning. Some psychological connection perhaps, in the exercise of hidden power.

Well now, these photographs were clearly to do with her work at Bowen's Gallery. Did I have the impression it was a very confidential relationship? Yes, these were archaeological photographs. Startling they were. The things must be worth a lot of money. Good condition. Mint condition, new-looking. There was a great golden cauldron. And a cup like the one I'd deposited bits of. Or so they were told. Yes, they did think to check that themselves. It was what I'd prophesied, wasn't it? Oh yes, of course they had notes of all those discussions with me. Even if one couldn't go into every point at once, notes were kept, and later they were most useful. Now would I like to see the photographs? It might help? Easier maybe if they came down to the Isle of Wight? If I didn't mind my holiday being interrupted? Oh, and had I heard of the burglary in

Oxfordshire? Ah, yes. Quite.

So that afternoon we met a plain-clothes officer at the hovercraft landing-area and drove him up to the old-fashioned hotel in Newport. The photographs were thrilling, and to make them more so, several of them were marked in pencil on the back: 'Carisbrooke', 'Carisbrooke?' and 'Not Carisbrooke'. I was assured the pencil writing was Tanner's or Touloupian's. They represented therefore the entire repertory from which he was choosing or had by now already chosen what was to come out of the ground at Carisbrooke. One print was even marked in so many words, 'Stoup, Carisbrooke'. They certainly represented dishonest dealing. All I could have wished them to have added was another set of photographs marked 'Iggleby, Stonehouses'. That might yet turn up.

There was now no more doubt in my mind about the trick and how it was to be worked. Nor could there remain any doubt that Katya was either very deeply in his confidence or attempting blackmail. Her disappearance had become sad and sinister. By now her photograph would be appearing on television. They had found an old photograph among the disorder of her possessions. It was taken some years ago for a modelling agency, a pathetic attempt at a new start. The police showed me a copy. She had looked older when I saw her, and her hair had been different. The likelihood that she tried blackmail and failed was increased by the burglary and the search of the terraced house in Fulham. In a house like that, no ordinary burglar would bother to search so thoroughly.

The photographs themselves were to me stupefying. Which of these things were real and which were not? I was away from books, I was floundering ridiculously among conjectures built upon conjectures. At least there was no doubt about the Dolphin Painter. Here he was again, with not one, but two complete vases, a cup and one of those tall jars called a bell-krater. The tall jar was nicely decorated with dolphins and columns. It was a fountain-house, a source of water built into a kind of scrawny black portico. Women came to it carrying water-pots. They were sketchily drawn. The water came from spouts in the shape of dolphins. That was why the dolphins seemed to be swimming between pillars.

The cup was not so careful. That is, it was even more careless than this painter's usual style. But surely genuine. All the more surely genuine. Satyrs chased around the outside of the cup, weapons at the ready in the war of love. Fixed bayonets, as it were. The ladies with those pine-cones on the top of sticks, and one of them with a lighted torch, ran away as fast as one can in an ankle-length dress in a Greek vase-painting. It was a world made for men. They were all going to be caught, but that was left to the imagination of the drinker. And when he drained his drink what did the drinker find in the bottom of his cup? An enormous, smug and smiling dolphin. Those two vessels must have cost Touloupian a small fortune. Very small, in the state of the market for Greek vases, but a few hundred pounds even in Egypt.

I was beginning to be angry, because I was wondering where these things really did come from, and where they were now. Would they surface again in Switzerland? In an American private collection? With these excellent photographs I could pursue them to the ends of the earth. But they were not necessarily stolen. They were certainly unknown pieces. I knew that because I had just worked through the recorded work of the Dolphin Painter. They had been robbed from a grave, illegally excavated. That would never be traced, now. In Italy? In Africa? Of course not Britain? The thought that I would never, never know made me very angry indeed.

There were two great bronze cauldrons like the one Ralph Iggleby had, with the same kind of simple and moving animal sculptures. This time it was horses, not cows. Mares, with foals suckling. Did they not drink mares' milk as well as cows' milk? The Iranians and the central Asian tribes drink mares' milk to this day. I believe that the buffet of the Trans-Siberian Express, which is committed by dogma to serving the food of the country it passes through, serves aerated mares' milk in Mongolia. Why not reindeer meat? It would be just as appropriate. The bronze cauldrons must surely be genuine. One had been patched, as bronze armour sometimes is. That was surely an ancient mend. The thing was an heirloom. Hallstatt is the beginning of the Iron Age, but bronze was still valued.

Several photographs showed weapons of iron. This was

clearly meant to be a very grand burial indeed. Sword, dagger, two spears. Some horse-harness in a tangle, obviously genuine, from where? That was marked on the back 'Not Carisbrooke'. Touloupian knew his limitations. The local native pots suggested that somewhere near here he had opened a real grave-mound. It was hideous to my eye, but there are those who love it, and I was certainly infuriated that games like this should be played with it. There was no doubt it was a game, because of the treasures of gold.

A gold chain of twenty links lay gleaming on a black velvet cloth. It was hard to imagine the scale, since none was indicated. These were not the photographs that were going to be produced later. These were a catalogue, a card-index of items. They were meant to be destroyed when the things went into the ground. In these photographs everything not genuine was in mint condition, as it was made but before the effect of age had been supplied. I do not know, because such things seldom come on the market, but I reckon that a solid gold chain that could claim to have come out of a distinguished ancient grave would multiply its value by ten. When you think what it would be worth in the first place, that comes to a lot of money. There were also two plain gold bowls.

But the masterpiece was more elaborate. It was extremely bold, and for a few moments I was taken in by it. It was outsize, because a silver sword lay against it. It must be some three feet high. It was a vast, enlarged version of the kind of pottery vessel in which the Greeks mixed crude wine with water for a party. It was made of solid gold. Around its neck Greeks and barbarians fought. Its handles were coiled, scaled, interwoven pythons. Under the heads of the snakes a boy on each side stood on his head, fully modelled, a young body arching outwards and anchored only by the hands below and the feet above, which were under the snakes' chins.

Somewhere, I had seen something like it in bronze. And the battle scene surely in a vase-painting. The snakes' heads had a rich, familiar look. It was all going to take a long, long time to check. If it had come out of the ground in a respectable excavation, I would have accepted it. Ancient or modern, it was somebody's masterpiece. It was intended for southern Greek, I suppose, from one of the Greek colonial cities of southern Italy. There was a touch of the Treasure of Vix about it, and a touch of a bronze water-pot in one of the Swiss museums. It was so baroque that it might almost be Etruscan. As a work of art, it was on the edge of being a triumph. As a studious pastiche, an essay on antiquity written in three dimensions, I found it engaging. The boy standing on his head, surely he was an old friend? Was he not the anthropomorphic handle of a famous southern Italian piece, stood upside down?

I did not for a moment think that Touloupian himself had made these things. He lacked the calibre. In his business he was essentially a salesman. These hoaxes of his were a saleman's tricks. The photographs represented things he had amassed or recently bought. I know too little about the techniques of forging pieces cast in bronze or in gold, but if one has access to numerous originals, including terracottas, can it be so very difficult? If my saying so inspires anyone else to attempt new works of art as magical as the Carisbrooke krater, as I suppose it would have been called, then I accept that responsibility. The trouble is not the making of such things, but the greed, and the lies, and the philistine disregard of archaeological propriety and historical truth.

By the time I had studied all the photographs, my feelings were mixed. I did still feel angry about what was planned, but the range and depth of the planning struck me with a kind of awe, an unwilling admiration. I was quite unable to fit together the dreadful and violent killing of old Ralph Iggleby, and the brutal and disgusting murder of Mary, with all this. When I tried to do so the things themselves seemed to me suddenly dirty. Ancient art history took on a sordid appearance. Perhaps the vicar was right. Perhaps one ought not to disturb the grave-mounds. Was that what the vicar had said?

I confirmed to the police what the photographs represented. Just such another tomb-group as Ralph Iggleby had found in Oxfordshire, with the unavoidable conclusion that they were both phoney, and that this second one was due to be discovered in the grave-mound behind the Rev Dr Stoup's bungalow.

'I think, sir, we shall have to have that open.'

'Oh don't do that for heaven's sake.'

'Why not sir?'

'I mean, do of course. But you'll damage it. After all, that is a real grave-mound I think.'

'And antiquity has its rights, sir?'

'Well, it has in a way.'

'All the same we'll have to have it open, sir. There's too many unknowns in this case and that's one we can get rid of.'

'There are ways and ways of opening it.'

'Who would you wish to have the overseeing of it, sir?'

'It really ought to be done by someone with experience of that sort of digging.'

'Would you be present yourself, sir? We'd have no objection to that.'

'I'm not an expert on Isle of Wight grave-mounds.'

'All we can do in the time, sir, I'm afraid.'

In the end I found myself booked for the next day. I did ask at the same time whether the police were watching Dr Stoup. They said they were. They hoped that possibly he might lead them to Tanner. I wondered very much, yet again, what terms those two were on.

18

The call came earlier than any of us expected. Joy was yawning and patting her night-clothes. I was pottering about in the way that men do, wondering where to put my cuff-links. The phone rang, and we stared at it in disbelief.

'Police here, sir.'

'Oh yes.' I was guarded.

'Trouble up at Carisbrooke, sir. Thought you might like to know. In fact we thought you might like to come along.'

'What is it?' I was more guarded than ever.

'Well it seems they may be going to open the mound. Looks like it. We should like you there. We'll send a car for you of course. Someone you know already.'

'Oh – er – what about Joy?'

'Sooner she didn't come if you don't mind. We think we've identified the two men who imprisoned you, and the one who followed her as well. Quite a gathering.'

'Oh I see.'

'Better she doesn't stir out of her bed, sir. And we shall have a man watching the hotel, just in case.'

'I'll come downstairs now.'

'Thank you sir. We'll be there in five minutes or so.'

Where on earth had I put my damned cuff-links? Where was my torch? I had a torch. Joy was not pleased with my adventuring off like that, not after the last adventure. But she consented in the end. The only condition she made was that I had to take a quarter of a bottle of brandy with me, and wake her up whatever time I got in.

My old friend the bald-headed officer of the other day came beaming into the hotel.

'Looks like we've got them this time, Mr Jonson. All the lot. We're just waiting our time.'

'What was it that warned you?'

'We had a man on the road, but I reckon Joe Biggleswade spotted him, when he took his dog for a walk, up by Dr Stoup's land. Joe would know a policeman, as the fox knows the hound, sir. So then we had dead quiet after that. Our man had nothing to report except Joe Biggleswade. But they've come over the hill, sir. Over the downs. They had to come right past the Castle, and that's where they were heard. We've had our reinforcements in there since morning. Fine place for overlooking, those battlements are. What they were made for.'

'And how many of them are up there?'

'There's the three Brighton bruisers, and there's two others we can't make out. Whether Touloupian's there I don't know. If I thought he was I should be tempted to arrest him now, because he's a dangerous man. But what evidence have we against him, so far? Only this kidnapping of you. And as to that, sir, if it comes to court and he has a clever lawyer, they'll make out you never really saw him in those trees. Or you had a grudge. That Rev Stoup will give evidence on his side I dare say. Swear he was somewhere else. Now mind how you go here, sir. There's a water-splash, but I think we'll leave the car, if you don't mind, and walk the last bit.'

'And then there's this opening of the mound, Mr Jonson. In itself that's not criminal. It's on private land and it's not a listed monument. It's hard to know what they really are up to, that's the truth of it. Of course if that Saintly had not done 'imself in, then we might have many answers. As it is, sir, it's more questions, isn't it?'

I said I thought one of the biggest questions now was what had become of Katya. Wherever she was she must know a great deal.

'Ah yes, them photographs. I heard about them. She's either with him now, sir, or they've done away with her, that's my opinion. But we shall have an end to it tonight. We shall rope them in tonight, come whatever.'

I was greatly comforted by this view of things, because it seemed to me that on a dark night with all the downs to wander over the fugitives would have an advantage over the pursuers. I nourished the cowardly hope that my two personal bruisers would run in any direction rather than mine. For the time being at least I was safe. The plan was to make no move until the other side made one. They were sitting on the hillside apparently waiting for someone to arrive, or was it for a signal to be given? They had crowbars, picks and shovels, and a sack. I had nothing but Ralph Iggleby's trowel from the car, and even that made me feel foolish.

We had crept up through the wards and courtyards of the Castle. The greyish stones had a hoary look in the dark. They were like rough, grey vegetation, petrified. Here and there they were coarsely eaten away by the rain. Stairs and ladders ran upwards and disappeared. Flywalks tottered over our heads. It was up one of these places that I was first led. The police thought, I suppose, that it would keep me of harm's way until the moment came for me to help with the mound. The flaw in the operation was that the villain might be acting within the law. Still, kidnapping would do for a holding charge, and the Stonehouses connection was likely to turn up more evidence with time.

The downs were dark and endless. I believe on a clear day you can see the sea from Carisbrooke. But not that night. I could make out little indeed. The wind blew over the grave-mounds on the hill-top, smelling faintly of sea-water, and that was all. Those few stars that glittered were soon covered over again by clouds that moved fast until they filled the sky. It was cold on the ramparts. Once or twice I saw lights flashing below me. I thought they were signals but I had no idea what they meant or who was signalling. The police seemed to be numerous; I could tell that from the transport in the Castle car-park. Nothing was moving on the roads.

At last up the road came a car. It was driving across the hills from the south of the island, from Shanklin or Ventnor perhaps. And at almost the same time a lonely cyclist appearing from nowhere, from the other direction. The car had stopped at the site of the vicar's bungalow. How many men got out? It was curiously hard to tell. Two at least, and a third who had to be helped. No, a bundle that had to be carried. A prisoner could it be? No, it was equipment of some kind. They had a wheelbarrow. A policeman appeared beside me. 'The inspector's compliments, sir, and he thinks you ought to be moving down now. We're sealing off the road there now behind that bicycle. You'll be quite safe up to that barrier, sir.'

I went down the walls of Carisbrooke Castle like an Indian monkey down a temple wall. I was directed across the car-park to a small gate and a path. In two minutes more I was down at road level, not very far from the place where Biggleswade and his dog had been, on the day I first explored the mound. The inspector was there with a little throng of policemen. He made a sign for complete silence. I could hear the car engine still turned on. They were using its lights. The beams of its headlights shone into the enclosed area. The bicyclist was just arriving.

I could hear them talking, and someone laughed. What on earth was that bundle lying across the wheelbarrow? There was a noise from behind us, a fearfully loud, rattling engine. Policemen began to look round. It was coming on at a pace, and it had headlights. The police barrier was just a pole across the road, but the headlights picked it up and the noise stopped. I could see now that it was the vast yellow bulk of a bulldozer.

Before I had time to put two and two together, the machine restarted. It gave a great roar and came forward fast with its shovel swinging down. I hardly had time to jump.

Falling into a hedge is such a special sensation that no other excitement obliterates it. Particularly at night, and this was a good stiff hedge with more prickles than leaves. It smelt intoxicating, and it was also full of insects. By the time I had picked myself up, a running fight was taking place all up and down the road. The bulldozer had come to a halt by the car with a great yell of 'Rozzers!' It was driven by Joe Biggleswade. He had not come to a halt on purpose. His aim was to drive on into the dark. But the police had pulled him off his machine and were now thumping him.

'I told you Joe Biggleswade,' (thump) 'last time I saw you,' (thump) 'that if you stepped out of line,' (thump) 'oh you would, would you?' (prolonged thumping).

The bruisers with the crowbars and shovels had made a first attempt to defend themselves on the slopes of the grave-mound. But the voice of a police loud-hailer from out of the dark behind them had scattered them, and the only two still left uncaptured when I saw them each had a little knot of uniformed figures close behind. One went over into a ditch and was taken. The other ran up on to the downs where he was surrounded and overwhelmed. One policeman was badly hurt by a crowbar. No fire-arms had been used.

One man and one only got away. It was because the car engine was still running. Touloupian was close to the car when the bulldozer smashed the barrier. He leapt like a startled night-animal, and in a moment he was away down the road into Newport. As he gathered speed he ran down the awkward figure of the cyclist. It was the Rev Dr Stoup. The vicar never spoke more than a few words again. He never recovered full consciousness. He lived three days with a face of nightmare. Then he died. During his last three days there was always a policeman by his bed. The only time the police ventured to question him, he replied only with an expression of pain, and the words, 'It doesn't matter now.' His sister offered to question him on their behalf, but he gave her the same answer.

Touloupian was pursued of course. More of that later. The

first thing that took my attention, as the fighting died down and the prisoners were taken away, was the upturned wheelbarrow and what had fallen out of it. The bald-headed inspector had seen it too. He bent down and slit open the sacking the parcel was wrapped in. The sacking shrouded the dead body of Katya. The gruesome end of another life, as embittered an end as Dr Stoup's, and in its terrible way as unproductive a life. I have heard blackmailers called the lowest of mankind. Standing there on that night, it was not what I felt.

What had been going on? To bury a dead body in an ancient grave-mound is intelligible enough. But why so many men and why the bulldozer? It had been their intention to clear the mound, to excavate it first, hence the tools, and then to flatten it and redistribute the earth, hence the bulldozer. They were not going to risk burying a dead girl in a mound which might one day be excavated. They were going to demolish the ancient grave and produce its skeleton. No one was going to resift that earth when the excavation was over. Katya's murdered body would be safe underneath those tons of earth.

Then why had Alfred Stoup called his mound Mount Ephraim? I was at a loss. Why had he declared with such passion it would never, never be excavated? Why had he talked about the dead? Was it possible he had not known or not understood or not approved of the plan? Could it be that his plan was to bury her in the mound as it stood, and to leave her after that, with the treasures of the mound to console her, to await doomsday? I voiced these suspicions to the bald-headed inspector.

'Well sir, we shall have to open that mound,' he said. 'And then we may know more.'

The new deposit was not deep down. I do not know any archaeologist whom it would have fooled, inexpertly buried as it was. It came out piece by piece, in no particular relationship, like sixpences out of a Christmas pudding. The only reason for proceeding at all carefully was that we might have done damage. And of course second burials did occur in ancient times at the top of existing grave-mounds. A new race of warriors passing by the graves of the ancient people would open the top like the top of an egg, and pop in their chief. But the original burial lies at the bottom of the mound, and when we had accounted for the levels of recent disturbance, we left the rest for tomorrow's light and the local archaeological society. You can see the finds now any time you like, in the Carisbrooke Castle Museum.

Our things were impressive as they came out in the light of torches and lamps. They were things of the dead in a true sense by now. I wished in a way that we had buried them all in that mound, all the dead of this horrible story as it unfolded. And that we had left the grave-goods buried with them. If that was the Rev Dr Stoup's intention, then I was beginning to see deeper into that strange clergyman. As he went down under the car he had cried out as wildly as King Lear. The gold had an evil gleam. It was not really very beautiful, only awfully heavy.

'There was no doubt,' I asked my police friend, 'that he ran over the vicar intentionally?'

'None sir. But you get the lawyers arguing over a thing like that and then you'll see the jury falling asleep, Mr Jonson. Believe me. I've seen 'em.'

As we left I asked him whose the antiquities and the forgeries were. He thought the coroner would have to decide. And of course the lawyers. They might in the end belong to old Alfreda Stoup, she being her brother's heir. The land was certainly his.

'And as for Touloupian, we have still to catch him I'm afraid.'

'What about the others? What will you charge them with?'

'Kidnapping. Attempted gbh. That's grievous bodily harm. Resisting the police in the execution of their duties. Making a public affray. Bit of burglary I shouldn't wonder. Theft of that van. And there'll be other things before we're through with it.'

'Not murder?'

'Accomplice maybe. I expect they knew all about it. I'm sure Joe Biggleswade did. But the rest of them? Suppose they say they knew nothing about the girl? I wonder if we can make it stick.'

'How was she killed? And how long ago?'

'They'll be going into that now, back at the station. He came in that car from the south of the island. A house there I suppose. We shall trace it through the car tomorrow morning. And it is tomorrow morning now, if you take my meaning. So

I'll say goodnight, Mr Jonson. One of these officers will drop you off at your hotel. And I hope they'll have Touloupian by now.'

But Touloupian smashed his car into a warehouse wall, driving too fast through Newport. He got away from there on foot, with two or three policemen pelting after him. What with the whistles blasting and the car crashing and half the wall collapsing and glass breaking and feet running in those boots they wear, they must have woken half the town. In the bottom of the town there are the old docks, and Touloupian headed into there. They were close by. The police must have thought they had him, because those docks are a dead end.

But it seems he had a motor launch ready. He would have used it that night anyway. He had it in midstream by the time the police came up, and then of course he was away in a cloud of fumes, like a mechanical monster. Of course they did catch him in the end, just as he got into Cowes. Had he been going to put in somewhere on the way? But the police were always too close behind him. It turned out later that he had a big motor yacht in the river Hamble. When they caught him he was aiming to cross over the Solent and disappear up beyond Warsash. Even had he got that far, he would have needed a new crew for his yacht, because the police had the old crew up at Carisbrooke.

It was on his boat that he was living, and that was where the girl was murdered and sewn up in sacking. She was shot with a gun they found in the cabin. And her murder was the only serious charge they could bring against Touloupian. The argument about the two digs would have meant a case of fraud, but fraud against whom? He hadn't attempted to sell anything. All the connections with the death of Ralph Iggleby were the merest suspicion. Cloudy vapours in the darkness of that night.

They even dropped the kidnapping charge in the end. It was too hard to prove against him. They substituted assault charges. Touloupian denied I was held on that hulk on his instructions. He maintained his orders had been misunderstood. He was tried for what he claimed was a crime of passion. For that he got five years of which he served three. The real punishment was losing his hoard of treasures. There was no way he could claim it without being publicly branded as a fraudulent antique dealer and worse. And he denied the writing on the photographs was his. So it all went in the end to Miss Alfreda Stoup.

19

The next missing piece of the puzzle fell into place when we got home. It was the day of Ralph Iggleby's funeral, and we were due there in the afternoon. We drove up in the morning, the old car made very good time, and we were passing my favourite scarecrow by eleven thirty in the morning. It stands shivering in some allotments not far from Newbury racecourse, dressed in old jockey silks. Or it used to be there, but recently I always seem to miss it. Horse-racing has survived although J-class ocean racing has died; that scarecrow means a great deal to me.

We stopped for lunch at a bistro in Little Clarendon Street, which is Oxford's Latin quarter, and Joy bought a dark dress. I had only a dark tie, which I acquired in the Isle of Wight. Before we left the city, I called at my college to pick up the post. There was a mountain of it. Books, pamphlets, official forms, bills and a few personal letters, mostly the kind that get forwarded between seven addresses from someone you met at a conference in Valparaiso. I took them out to the car. Joy was driving, and as we nosed our way north along a long tunnel of Victorian fortifications and flowering trees, I opened the personal letters.

One of them had a local postmark. It was carefully written in rather fine old-fashioned writing, learnt in a village school in the days when village schools were parish schools. The core of what they taught you was very careful writing, and the rest was a way of life that went with it. The letter was from Mary. It was the last letter she wrote, the one she was taking to the post on the day she was murdered. It read:

Dear Mr Jonson,

I am writing you this letter because I need to talk to you, to tell you about things here. But I have no opportunity now, with Mr Iggleby gone and who knows about these Prouters. Mrs Prouter is a fine lady I'm sure, and talks and talks. Mr Iggleby called her the Spouter. By name and by nature. But I will see things done properly and the blinds down for Mr Iggleby which she did not wish. And remarks she made about you also, about you and Joy. I say enjoy yourself while you are young which I never did, and Mr Iggleby would say the same. He was wise, so sir and Miss Joy congratulations.

I am writing to relieve my conscience of worry. There is things going on I do not understand. On the night he died Mr Iggleby was expecting someone and he was expecting to have trouble. This he told me, it is not my habit to pry, but I am glad I know though I have told no one. Mr Ralph was angry and it was about his pots and things he dug up. He said that cow was screwed on wrong or soldered on wrong and it was not right. It looked all right to me, but he said no and he was very wise sir. He said you would know too, and this is why I am telling you, in case you have not seen.

Well, that night when he died he was expecting to be angry with someone. He had been playing with his pots as I say, studying them he called it, and he had that letter from Doctor Saintly about them. And I have it on my conscience that I believe Burr had told Doctor Saintly that the will was altered and he was not getting any of the pots and nor was the vicar. Burr had told it to my friend and my friend told me. I think that this is at the root of someone murdering Mr Ralph, but I know he was also angry and he could have fired first. He could never have hit anyone with that thing, not to hurt, he was like a little boy with it.

Well sir, I am telling you that Burr says he has told them all that evening they was getting nothing. But he meant the doctor. After I have posted this off to you, which you will have tomorrow morning sir, in your college, where you work, I am going to talk to the vicar. It will relieve my mind.

With best respects and service

Your Mary

We had to stop the car on the edge of Oxford so that I could read it to Joy. It had probably taken some days to arrive; that does happen whatever kind of stamp you use. But even if it had reached me the next morning, Mary would have been already dead.

It left little doubt about the murderer, but some about the murder. It must have been John Saintly who quarrelled so violently with Ralph Iggleby. He had nothing to gain except avoiding exposure for a silly fraud. Would he mind so much about that? And yet the vicar knew Tanner. Given Tanner's ambitious plans, whoever was in the one plot must have been in the other. That meant John Saintly and Alfred Stoup were both in it from beginning to end. And Mary had written, 'I am going to see the vicar and talk to him.'

Was the alibi in some appalling way the truth? Doctor Saintly really was with the vicar that afternoon? They must have had many anxious conferences, so why not one that afternoon? Mary's revolting murder followed immediately. For my money that was the sabre-swinger, the doctor. The vicar could swing a heavy axe. Could, but did not. Or had the doctor sent the vicar in to Ralph Iggleby, knowing how deeply wild and perhaps how mad he was? We did not think so. He would not have trusted him so far. Then the vicar was a witness, and a guilty witness, of what happened to Mary. The nervous collapse may easily have been real. And the attempt to silence him for ever was a panic reaction. Saintly must have feared involuntary betrayal as well as genuine repentance. It was Saintly by that time who was going mad.

Ralph Iggleby and Mary were buried at the same time. The words of the funeral service were as they always are. The church was packed. I find country funerals comforting on the whole, but there are parts of the service that send a chill down my spine. I saw Mrs Prouter glaring at Joy and me, but I resisted the temptation to show her Mary's letter. Most people were very nice to us afterwards. I did show the letter to a policeman, who said, 'Hm,' and took it away with him. That day was a forlorn ending to this saga of violence and escape. The pleasure had gone out of the chase, and out of archaeology for me. It would come back but in some new context I was not able to foresee. It would be clean of association.

We went to the house afterwards for a glass of sherry with the Prouters. It was a cold, awkward ceremony, worse than the double funeral. At least outside there were people crying real tears and sniffing into handkerchiefs. For the Prouters, the sherry and sandwiches were a first opportunity to meet many of their new neighbours. For Joy it was a black, black day. For me it was a sad excursion.

We walked back across the park for the last time, to where we had left the car beside the church. The grass was a vivid, strange green, and the trees looked so old, and the leaves so soft, and the sky so ominous, that I had the impression it was going to snow and blot out the year.

'Can it snow,' I asked Joy, 'so late in the year?'

'Oh yes,' she said. 'It can snow in June.'

'I think it may be going to.'

'So do I.'

20

What a mistake it is to dine in other people's colleges. Joy was sitting tranquilly at home, eating eggs baked inside tomatoes, with fresh chives and I dare say cream. She would have some attractive feature propped up that she was still reading from yesterday's paper. When I got in she would look up and smile and say 'Back already?' It was my night for the committee with Frowser. We had pursued the phantom originals of the classics through translations of translations of translations. I held out for *Horestes*, which starts with the stage direction 'Enter Rusticus and Hodge upon the Battlements of Mycenae'. Frowser wanted a version of *Iphegenia in Aulis* I had never read. He said the translator, a learned lady writing in 1564 or so, sometimes spells the name Iphigeneia, which shows that she knew Greek.

155

I had steered clear of our last conversation, and so had he. There was not a shred of evidence against him. He might even be innocent. But suddenly, over the port and nuts, he leant towards me and opened the subject. There were not many of us dining, so although port always separates you as far as possible from your host, we were all huddled together in a little group.

'Ralph Iggleby's death,' he announced.

I fell silent.

'You were deeply involved in that from beginning to end I understand.'

'You could put it like that.'

'And your feelings. Much stirred I thought.'

'More the more I think about it.'

'My friend Iggleby?' put in someone from the shadows. A face leaned forward. It was the expert on moated granges.

'Sad thing, what? Glad you were stirred. Hraa. Ralph Iggleby. Hrmm. Funny fellow in some ways. Kept daffodils in his moat.'

'Tell me Frowser,' I asked, 'have you known Tanner all his life?'

'Tanner? Oh, so you know that. Well then you understand more than I thought you did. Or you ought to.'

'Have you known him continuously?'

'On and off.'

'Was that how you met Alfred Stoup?'

'Dr Stoup? The vicar. Yes. And Miss Stoup. He was called Alfred was he?'

'Was Tanner a friend of theirs from school?'

'Friend? Then you still don't know? I should hardly call him a friend.'

'Why not? Don't know what?'

'It was known in the island, so I believe. Tanner was an orphan. His father was a sailor. Just disappeared. Miss Stoup was his mother. Dr Stoup was his uncle.'

'Really?'

'Mm. Have a nut.'